TENTS, TRAILS, & TURMOIL

A Camper And Criminals Cozy Mystery

Book Eleven

BY
TONYA KAPPES

TONYA KAPPES
WEEKLY NEWSLETTER

Want a behind-the-scenes journey of me as a writer?
The ups and downs, new deals, book sales, giveaways and more? I share it all! Join the exclusive Southern Sleuths private group today! Go to www.patreon.com/Tonyakappesbooks

As a special thank you for joining, you'll get an exclusive copy of my cross-over short story, *A CHARMING BLEND.* Go to Tonyakappes.com and click on subscribe at the top of the home page.

"What's this?" She picked it up.

"A Sierra Club brochure with Yaley Woodard's business card attached," I said between gulps of water. "Skip told me Yaley Woodard was supposed to have come to his business with a list of tours they booked and she never showed." I downed what was left in the water bottle and tossed it into the trash. "I told him she went missing a few days ago."

"No one tried to contact him?" Dottie questioned.

"You'd think they'd go through her client list and send someone out to check on them until she turns up." I shook my head and went back to my desk to see what messages Dottie had taken for me. "I also asked him if he'd smelled anything dead. Of course he hadn't, and I didn't see or smell anything either, but as soon as we got back to the opening of the trail, I smelled it again. We've got to find that dead animal."

I glanced over to see what all the noise Dottie was making was about. She was shuffling through her top desk drawer with a determined look on her face.

"Ah-ha!" She held up a box of matches with a big ole smile on her face. "I've got an idea."

"Does your idea have to do with smoking?" I guessed.

"With smoke." Her eyes grew. "Come on out here. I'm gonna show you an old hunter's trick."

"I can't wait to see this," I muttered and put the stack of messages back down on my desk.

We walked out of the office, and sure enough, that smell had wafted past us.

"Watch this." Dottie struck the match. The smell of sulfur filled the air around us as the flame exploded from the small stick.

Dottie held it up in the air. The light breeze sent the smoke of the match to the left before blowing it out.

"Did you smell the dead animal?" she asked as she took out another match.

"No." I took a couple of whiffs. "Oh gosh." I fanned my hand in front of my nose. "I do now."

Dottie quickly lit the next match, and the smoke blew the other way.

"Follow the smoke," she said.

With a pinched nose, we followed it, and it led us right to our dumpster.

"Oh my gosh." I couldn't stop laughing. "It's our dumpster. Didn't they come and empty it this week?"

"They did, but we've got to get Henry to clean it with bleach and water." Dottie waved her hand in front of her face. "Or better yet, get a new one."

"Gross." I took a deep breath through my mouth and gripped the handle of the small opening to peek inside just in case I could see exactly what the stink was. "Dottie," I gulped when I looked inside and saw a pair of shoes attached to some legs. "We don't need to call the garbage company. We need to call the police."

CHAPTER ONE

T he sun was shining brightly over my old Kentucky home.
I stood with my coffee from Trails Coffee Shop in my hands as I looked out over the grassy median that divided Main Street of downtown Normal, Kentucky.

"It's gorgeous, isn't it?" Violet Rhinehammer had walked up behind me, also admiring the tinted blue of the grass, rightly naming Kentucky the Bluegrass state. There was a vivid blue with a hint of green. "Who would ever think that in such a lovely town someone could be snatched up?"

Slowly I turned my chin to the side and looked at Violet. My eyes went wide-open as the word she chose to use, *snatched*, sent a shiver down my spine.

"Maybe right from the very spot you are standing in." Her brow took a jump, arching up into her forehead, minus any wrinkles from the Botox injections she regularly got. "How does that make you feel?"

"Three, two, one," I heard a man call from behind her.

Violet turned on a dime, and before I knew what was going on, Violet had dragged me into her situation.

"Coming to you live from downtown Normal, Kentucky in the heart of the Daniel Boone National Forest, where it is believed that thirty-one-year-old Yaley Woodard was snatched." Violet spoke with clear and concise words. She stared into the lens of the camera the cameraman was holding as if she weren't just talking to me.

This was why so many people loved and watched Violet on her news broadcasts. It was as if she were standing in your living room and talking directly to you. Honestly, it was a gift she had, and I tried to slip out of the shot. She grabbed me, not batting an eye once my way or taking her gaze off the camera. She held me in her grip, like prey.

"Right here, on this very spot, is the last time that video camera spotted Yaley with two cups of coffee in her hand. Two." Violet's tone turned eerie. "One for her and perhaps one for her abductor?"

The cameraman panned the camera up toward the newly placed security cameras that were an upgrade from the previous ones. We'd also just gotten an upgrade in the internet and wireless service all across the national park with the extra park state funding. A much-needed improvement.

"I'm standing here with Maybelline West, the owner of the Happy Trails Campground." Violet turned to me for the first time since the camera started to roll. Her long blond hair swept across her shoulder. It looked like it came out of one of those shampoo commercials. All dramatic-like. "Maybelline," she called me by my full name.

"Mae," I corrected her.

"Mae, tell me, how do you think this abduction is going to influence your business as the owner of a very popular campground for tourists who come to the national park?" She shoved the microphone up to my mouth, her eyes twinkling as they danced around my face.

"This is the first I'm hearing about the abduction, so there's no need to interview me, Violet." I gave her a smile and took a sip of my coffee, trying not to get lost in her drama, which she was at getting me to do.

"We are live." Violet batted her long eyelashes with a big smile as the words "We are live" put more fear in me than when she mentioned the word "snatched."

I glared at her and took a gulp of coffee, nervously tucking a strand of my curly hair behind my ear. It was out of control because I didn't try to tame it when I got out of bed just about an hour ago.

"I'm sorry. I'm not familiar with the abduction, so I honestly have no comment on how this news will affect my campground, Happy Trails Campground, here in Normal, Kentucky." I took the opportunity for a shameless plug since Violet decided to spring this impromptu interview on me, which I'm sure was not by coincidence, by the way.

"Yaley Woodard, a thirty-one-year-old female, had taken a lunch break. It is believed she was coming here to meet up with her boyfriend, Joel Grassle. She didn't return to work." Violet spoke in that on-air personality voice. "As you can see by the flyer put out by her brother, Ted Woodard, the family is worried. It's been seventy-two hours since someone last spoke to Yaley. This is not common behavior. This is not good for the tourism in Normal. What are your thoughts on that?"

She held the microphone back up to my face and handed me the missing person flyer she was talking about. It was the first one I'd seen.

"My prayers are with the family in the recovery effort," I started to say.

"Recovery effort? Do you know something we don't know since you are the girlfriend of Detective Hank Sharp?" If she shoved that microphone in my face one more time, I was going to club her with it.

Of course Violet had to bring that up. It was no secret and probably the reason for the tension always between us. Although we'd come together on a couple of occasions when one needed something from the other, she had tried to get her claws into Hank a few times to make him her own. When it became apparent that he and I were a strong couple, she'd retracted those claws but used every opportunity she could to get information out of me for her newscast and her newspaper articles, not to mention the various other magazines she contributed to.

"I-I didn't mean recovery..." I stammered to find the right words, which I was never good at when put on the spot.

"And as you can see, Ted Woodard is working tirelessly to get the word out." Violet lost interest in me and hurried off down the sidewalk past the downtown shops toward a man who was taping flyers on the carriage lights lining the median.

My focus went from the amazing sunny day we were having to the looming cloud over the top of Violet's head with the news of the abduction. I looked down at the flyer.

The woman staring back at me had a nice, warm smile. One of her front teeth slightly overlapped the other. Her face was thin, and though the photo was black and white, she appeared to have nice dark eyes and dark hair. There was a small heart-shaped charm dangling from a necklace around her neck. At closer look, the heart appeared to be outlined in small diamonds, and the chain was not simple. It was small hearts linked together to form the gold chain. The flyer even stated how Yaley would have on the heart necklace as an identifier. Apparently, she never took it off. I smiled at the license plate number. It read Tours and was one of those fancy license plates you had to pay extra for.

Immediately, I wondered who gave her the necklace and if, by chance, it was Joel Grassle.

The flyer said she worked at the Sierra Club as a tour guide. She had gone on a tour the day she disappeared. She had gone to lunch but only had an hour because they were having a meeting on the upcoming season tour schedule. The paper also claimed Yaley's car was missing. There was a five-thousand-dollar reward for any information, along with the Normal Police Department's phone number printed at the bottom.

I looked up when I heard some footsteps.

"Mornin'." Alvin Deters stood outside of his shop, Deters Feed-N-Seed.

He gave me the good ole Baptist nod and fumbled with his key ring until he found the key to open the door. His cowboy hat was pulled down over his eyes, creating a shadow down his face. "Sad news. I heard it on the radio on my way into town."

Alvin had on his usual outfit, even in the warm weather. A plaid shirt tucked into dark-blue jeans with his big silver belt buckle shined to a sparkle.

"Yeah." I gave one last glance toward Violet before I turned my attention back to Alvin, following him into the shop. "I hope she's okay."

"Me too." He flipped the sign on the door to Open and flipped on the lights. "What brings you out so early this morning?"

"I have a whole new group of campers coming in for the weekend, and I need to get some supplies. I've got to get the bungalows all cleaned up since I'd closed them down for the winter." I looked around the shop to see what direction I wanted to go first. "Mainly the necessities."

The necessities being batteries of all varieties, a couple of new flash-lights, night-light bulbs, coffeepot filters, cleaning supplies to restock all the bungalows' linen closets, shampoos, along with some tooth-brushes, toothpaste, and all the accouterments. Not that I was obligated to provide those—we sold baskets of such items in the office—but it was the kindness and added touch that made staying at Happy Trails Campground a memorable experience.

My shoulders tensed, my teeth bore down together, and I could feel my shoulders rising toward my ears. A sure sign of stress.

"You okay?" Alvin called from the counter. He'd taken his cowboy hat off and exposed his light-brown hair, which was pretty full for an older man like Alvin. Well... older than me.

If I recalled correctly, when I moved to Normal, I'd heard he was in his fifties. I guessed every one of us was getting older as the years ticked by, and that's exactly what time had done for me in the past couple of years since I'd made Normal my home.

"I'm good." I bent my head down to study the variety pack of batteries to make sure they were all ones I could use. I had scads of these packs where I didn't need all the C batteries, but the flashlights I had picked up appeared to need C batteries. "Did you happen to know Joel was dating the missing girl?"

I was having a hard time concentrating on what I had come into the Feed-N-Seed to purchase. Yaley's dark eyes haunted me, and I couldn't help but wonder where she had gone, if she'd gone. Maybe Joel was a good source to ask. Maybe Yaley had some sort of dark secret or needed to get away from town for a little bit.

Hank and I, and the dogs of course, had just returned from a nice little beach vacation because we needed to get away. The same could be said for Yaley.

"He'd mentioned he'd gone out on a few dates with a new girl, but he didn't mention who. Who told you he was dating her?" Alvin asked.

"Violet." I peered over my shoulder and out the window of the shop to see if Violet was still doing her live segment for the news.

"She should know. She's pretty good at getting to the source." Alvin walked out from behind the counter, headed back to the two swinging doors, and disappeared behind them.

He was right about Violet. She did have a way to get to the sources, and if her source about Joel was right, I'm sure Hank already knew and had questioned Joel.

I walked around the different aisles, hoping my eyes would catch something I'd placed on my mental list, but really the only things that stuck out were batteries and flashlights.

Alvin came back, pushing a cart filled with sacks of seed, and refilled the gardening area while I continued to mosey around.

"You ready?" he called out when I walked up to the counter and put the items down.

"I guess so," I said and strolled about looking at the various items he had in the bins underneath the counter. "Bug spray." I clapped my hands in delight with the fact I recalled one more item on my mental list.

"Huh?" Alvin wiped his hands down his shirt to get off any loose seeds from the bags.

"I really need to write things down. I had a slew of things I wanted to buy and completely forgot." I shrugged and took out my wallet from my crossbody bag.

"If you remember, call me, and I'll set them aside." Alvin had been so good to me over the past couple of years. Even when he didn't need to be.

My now-dead ex-husband, Paul West, had taken half of the American population's money during a Ponzi scheme. Maybe not half, but it sure did seem like it, and it was millions. In fact, it was how I'd ended up in Normal and owning a campground while living in the RV. The only thing Paul had in my name and the government couldn't seize. A run-down campground. The RV was even worse.

Alvin Deters was one of the men Paul had conned. When I first came to town, most of the people in Normal had trusted Paul, and all of them ended up with nothing. That's when I decided not to sell the campground for a quick buck and fixed it up with the help of Alvin Deters, who generously loaned me items until I paid him back. And through a lot of social media work, advertising, and smart business, I brought the tourism industry back to Normal.

"Thank you, Alvin." I gave him the cash in exchange for the bag. "You've always been so good to me."

"You're easy to be good to." He winked. "Be careful, she might get you again." He pointed out the front window of the shop.

Violet and her cameraman were walking through the median and looked to be coming back.

In the distance, Ted Woodard was using a staple gun to hang the missing person flyers up on the large oak trees that stood on each side of an amphitheater and covered seating area.

The thick white pillars, like the ones you'd see on the front porch of a plantation home, that held up the amphitheater already had the flyers posted on them. It looked like he'd strategically placed the flyers under the gas lanterns as though they were spotlights. The twinkly lights danced around the poles.

My eyes drifted to the large ferns that the beautification committee had planted in the ceramic planters.

I walked out of Deters Feed-N-Seed, stood out on the sidewalk, and tossed my empty coffee cup in the trash can. I watched Violet to see what her next move was going to be. The cameraman pointed down Main Street toward the Smelly Dog, which was a pet groomer, and the Normal Diner. When he said something to Violet, it must've agreed with her because she nodded her head, and they nearly sprinted across the street.

Out of curiosity, I followed them down to the Normal Diner, where they'd already found seats at the counter.

I plopped down on the stool next to Violet.

"Well?" I questioned. "What did he say?"

"What did who say?" She swiveled the stool seat around to look at me.

"Ted, Yaley's brother. Don't act like I didn't see you." I gave Ty Randal a short nod when he walked by with the coffeepot in his hand and lifted it to me, his way of asking if I wanted some coffee.

"You didn't seem too interested earlier." Her eyes narrowed. "Why the change of heart?"

"Maybe I wasn't interested because look at me." I gestured down my body. "What part of this outfit did you think was great for television?"

The bleached, blotted Normal, Kentucky sweatshirt that I'd purchased when I first rolled into Normal a couple of years ago had seen better days. Not to mention how I destroyed it when I washed it at the Laundry Club Laundromat because I put too much bleach in the washer.

I was trying to kill off any sort of germs the RV had on my drive from New York City to Normal. The RV was so gross that it looked like a petri dish of illness.

"Mae, someone is missing. Do you honestly think the viewing public is going to look at your outfit?" Her shoulders slumped, and her eyes softened. "Okay, yeah. I do recall a few people I've interviewed who didn't have their teeth in or were dressed in pajama pants, but you're gorgeous."

"Don't butter me up." I picked up the hot cup of steaming coffee. After a nice long whiff of the fresh brew, I said, "Does he really think someone took her?"

"He said she's never called in for work. Never missed a day. She's always been early for meetings." Violet looked at me like I had some plausible explanation.

"What?" I asked with some hesitation.

"I don't know. You left Perrysburg when you were eighteen with no trace. Middle of the night, jumped on a Greyhound bus, only to be seen back in Kentucky twelve years later." She had a point. "You tell me, what is in Yaley's mind to have wanted to skip town, if she did?"

"I guess it would be different for everybody." I took a couple more sips and placed the cup back down on the counter. "For me, I was trying to escape my past. Every time I looked around Perrysburg, I was reminded of my family or how awful high school was. I knew I could do whatever I wanted when I became an adult. So at eighteen, stroke of midnight, I became the adult and took action to make my life better."

"But Yaley, why would she leave? I mean, there are no signs of her car. So she could've, but why?" Violet had put on her investigative reporter's thinking cap.

"Her brother said she was always reliable, right?" I wanted to make sure I had the facts right. Violet confirmed with a hard nod and a raised brow, encouraging me to go on with my theory. "Maybe she was tired of that life. Maybe she wanted to live a little more freeing life."

"But she didn't tell anyone?" Violet was having a hard time wrapping her brain around the concept I had about why Yaley left.

"Trust me." I let out a long sigh. "When you want to leave the life you are living, you'll do whatever it takes to get out of town. You never know," I muttered and picked the cup back up. "She might show up in a few days or a few weeks. Maybe she'll call someone tonight if she sees your broadcast."

"That's what Ted is hoping." Violet twisted her stool back around and looked out into the distance like she was thinking about what I'd said. "I just wonder who was close enough to her to know what she was thinking."

Violet wasn't being too good of an investigative reporter. There was one person that immediately came to my mind.

Joel Grassle.

CHAPTER TWO

There wasn't a telephone pole that I could see on my drive back to Happy Trails Campground that didn't have one of Yaley's missing person flyers stapled to it. Ted Woodard had covered each one with missing person flyers, including the big wooden electrical poles on the curvy forest road.

The bright sun burst through the windshield of my little car, and I couldn't help but wonder if Yaley was enjoying the sunshine while everyone who loved her was desperately trying to find her.

I turned right into the campground and drove underneath the wooden sign with HAPPY TRAILS CAMPGROUND neatly scrolled across it. The stress of thinking about Yaley seemed to melt as I took in the scenery of my beautiful campground.

The spattering of the sun's rays danced along the pavement through the trees, and the backdrop of the Daniel Boone National Forest mountains was laid out like a painting. All the bluegrass stood nice and thick, giving way to the various patches of Kentucky wildflowers that gave a little color to the vast pastures.

I'd pretty much kept all of the campground's buildings when I revitalized the place. The storage units were located on the right and were mainly used by the seasonal campers, who had rented year-round lots from me. The small building located in front of the storage units with the glass door that read OFFICE was where I spent most of my time.

Dottie Swaggert sat outside of the office in one of the folding chairs with a plastic crisscross seat that'd seen better days. A couple of the straps were broken with frayed edges. Her heinie pressed between the remaining bulging straps.

She raised her hand in the air to wave at me. Smoke swirled up around her as she blew out smoke from the cigarette nestled in between her lips. I waved back and pulled into one of the office parking spaces.

"Good mornin'! You're out awfully early." She drew in a big breath. The tip of her cig lit up bright red like her hair color as she sucked in.

She took another long draw before she butted it out on the ground and placed it in the ashtray by her feet.

"I wanted to get a jump on supplies for the bungalows," I said through the open window and grabbed the bag from the passenger seat. "Anything going on?" I asked.

Dottie Swaggert was the property manager long before I knew I was the owner. She literally knew everything and taught me about campers, campgrounds, the Daniel Boone National Forest, and all the people who lived in and around us.

"Glad to see you dressed for work." My brow twitched as I looked at the satin blue pajamas and furry slippers, not to mention her pink sponge curlers knotted all over her short red hair.

"I've still got fifteen minutes until I have to clock in. I came over to get my pot of coffee started, so it'd be good, hot, and ready when I came into work." She stood up and straightened up to her five-foot-nine frame. She stretched her arms above her head and twisted her shoulders left and then right. Her nose wrinkled and she took a few whiffs of air. "Do you smell that?"

A look of disgust crossed her face.

"Cigarettes. That's all I smell," I noted when I walked past her.

"Something got ahold of something out there. I smell it. Dead."

I followed her eyes as they looked into the woods.

"Well, we do live in the middle of the forest. There are bears, coyotes, skunks, squirrels, deer…" I could've gone on and on. I opened the door to the office. Dottie followed me in.

Before I shut the door behind me, I stuck my nose out the door and did get a little whiff of something.

"If I have time today, I'll take Fifi on a walking trail and see if we can find it," I told her and took the batteries and flashlights over to the supply closet. "First, I want to get the bungalows all aired out, fresh linens on the bed, make sure the dishes are ready to go."

Dottie grabbed the dry-erase marker off her desk and started to make a list on the hanging dry-erase board. Normally, the board had guests' names on it to welcome them when they came into the office to sign their rental agreement or had a listing of activities going on around the campground. Since we were in the late spring season heading right on into summer, the board would soon be filled with festivals, tour discounts, and the monthly party we hosted here at Happy Trails for the guests and members of the community.

But today, we were going to get that list of chores done.

The office door opened. Henry Bryan, my campground handyman, meandered in. No hurry whatsoever. Henry was a little scragglier in his appearance, but he was clean and a good worker. He had a big nose and wide smile that exposed the missing top two front teeth.

"Shooweee dawg." His country accent was an octave higher with him pinching his nose. "Something has died out there." He let go of his nose, shut the door, and fanned his face.

He had on his typical work uniform—one-piece blue zip-up overalls and the metal pole he used for stabbing trash he'd find as he walked around the campground.

"I told Mae that," Dottie said, taking credit.

"And I told Dottie I'd take Fifi on a hike this afternoon and see if we spot something." Though nature pretty much took care of itself, I did like to take advantage of the various hiking trails located around the campground, and going for a nice hike with my dog would be a way to find the odor.

"You better hope no one is checking in today because it's nasty out there," Henry continued before he noticed the coffeepot. "Who else wants a cup?"

"I do." Dottie was writing other things that needed to get done today before the new guests arrived. Neither of them even noticed or mentioned Dottie's dress attire. "Henry, I need you to look at the bottom of the paddleboats to make sure there's no pond scum on them. There's a loose board on the pier, so be sure to either replace it or nail it down good."

"What about the games in the recreation room?" I asked since summer brought a lot of families to the campground. With families, there were kids.

I'd found that kids most often got bored with sitting around a campfire and often got cranky from long hikes, so the arcade-style recreation room was great. It was loaded with video games, a ping pong table, dart boards, board games galore, and puzzles, along with vending machines loaded up with sugary treats.

The recreation room was also where I put out treats from local small businesses. The Cookie Crumble Bakery donated freshly made donuts, and Trails Coffee Shop supplied the coffee. It was also a great place for Mary Elizabeth, my foster mom, and Dawn Gentry, her business partner, to let the guests sample various goodies from the Milkery, their dairy farm, which was much more than just a dairy farm.

After I'd seen the devastation to the people of Normal that Paul had created, I set myself on a mission for the community to give back to one another. Love up on one another. My way of doing that was to bring as much of their business to the campground as I could.

"The recreation room is good to go." Henry took a gulp of his coffee. "I can get all the windows of the bungalows open, so when you get around to fixin' up them fancy beds and bathrooms, you can shut them."

"Sounds good." I couldn't help but smile, remembering the first time Henry and Dottie had walked into one of the bungalows after I'd finished redecorating them. The only reason I didn't rent them during the winter and early spring was because they didn't have heat.

They were little cabin-type structures that were nestled in the back of the campground and away from all the campers and lots that lined the lake that was located in the middle of the campground. We also had wooded lots for the guests who really wanted to be secluded.

The bungalows were a hit for the guests who wanted to think they were camping, but I'd call it more glamping. They were mostly rented for honeymooners, family reunions, and bridal parties. The bungalows varied from two to three bedrooms. Each had kitchens fully stocked with utensils. I did put little extras in them like coffee, a welcome pack with fresh fruit, and a bottle of wine. I also made sure each bathroom had neat little homemade hand soaps from the small boutiques around the Daniel Boone National Forest as well as various pieces of furniture made by artists from the area.

The bedding was actually bought and shipped from different places around the states. I was a stickler for a good bed and comfortable bedding, so I made sure my guests loved it too.

It was the little touches of southern hospitality and comfort that made Happy Trails Campground stick out from the hundreds of other campgrounds in the park and made guests come back over and over again.

If it were up to Dottie and Henry, they'd throw a pack of hot dogs in the refrigerator and a sleeping bag on the bed and call it good.

"I've got to run back into town later to pick up the bedding from Betts, so it'll be much later in the day." I wanted to give Henry a timeline so he could do his other jobs. There was never a lack of jobs to do around here.

"That'll give me time to get all the kindlin' next to the lots." He nodded and refilled his mug again. "I'll stack a little wood up near the campfire sites too. We got a lot of down trees from the ice storm this winter."

"Sounds like a plan." I smiled and looked in the closet at the various baskets we offered for purchase. "Dottie, do we have a list of baskets ordered?"

"I do." She exchanged the dry-erase marker for the file on her desk with the new guests' contracts. She opened it. "Bungalow one is a honeymoon, and he ordered the spa package for his new wife."

Henry took his coffee and walked out of the office but not without a groan and mentioning something about the awful smell.

I took out the spa gift basket that included a robe, slippers, massage oils, candles, facial masks, chocolates, and wine. All the items were from local businesses as well. By creating the baskets and selling them, it was another way to get local businesses into the minds of my guests. It worked too.

After this couple tasted this wine, I'm sure they'd go schedule a tour with the Sierra Club...Sierra Club...

"Say"—I held the basket in my arms—"who is the rep you use for the Sierra Club?" I asked Dottie.

Since she was the local expert in the office, I let her handle all the contact between the local events and tours.

"Yaley Woodard." Her words made my jaw drop.

"I was afraid of that." My brows furrowed. "I heard today that she's been missing for a couple of days."

"Missing?" Dottie's head jerked back.

"Yeah. Apparently she was at work, did a tour, went to lunch, and never came back." I shrugged and walked over to hand her the basket.

"Well, that's not like her." Dottie shuffled some papers around her desk before she finally found the desk calendar. "You know, she was supposed to come here yesterday with the new tour schedule. She never showed. I just remembered that. Where do they think she went?"

"I have no idea. Her brother was posting up flyers all over downtown this morning. And Violet Rhinehammer was doing a story on it." I failed to mention how Violet had caught me off guard, on camera. Dottie would never let me live it down.

"Huh." Dottie grabbed the TV remote and turned the TV on.

"I'm going to head on out to get ready and take Fifi for her walk," I told Dottie, but she was glued to the TV just as Violet had come on to do the repeat segment. "Bye!"

The day was too pretty to drive the short distance to my parked RV, so instead of driving, I decided to walk. The breeze whipped up, sending a whiff of the dead animal straight up my nose. On a dime, the wind shifted, and the smell was gone. It was nasty, but the view of the campground made all that go away.

There was a road around the lake with concrete pads, a grassy area, a campfire setup, and all the hookups anyone needed for whatever recreational vehicle they parked at Happy Trails. We accepted all makes and models of RVs, which some campgrounds in the Daniel Boone National Forest didn't. Believe it or not, there was snobbery in the RV world.

In fact, there were some parks that didn't allow any recreational vehicles older than ten years old on their property. And not all RV campgrounds provided all the hookups like Happy Trails. I was happy to host anyone as a guest, and I hoped they felt that way too.

The feeling of community was something that I'd craved all my life, and owning the campground did that for me.

The sparkling blue water on the lake rippled underneath the ducks' feet as they glided across the water. They looked like they were swimming with ease, but I knew their little feet under the water were paddling so fast. It made me think of Yaley.

On the surface, she was well organized, put together, and appeared to be happy. But like the ducks' feet, how did she really feel underneath her skin where no one could see? Had she had her breaking point and simply took off, just like I did so many years ago?

The sounds of laughter and footsteps came from one of the many trails around the campground and brought me out of my thoughts. No one emerged from the trails, so they were just passing by and not guests of Happy Trails.

My RV was actually very adorable. My little yellow home on wheels was perfect for me and Fifi. It had a pop-up roof that made for extra space, and I'd completely redone the entire inside.

There was a kitchen, bathroom, and one bedroom, which made plenty of space for me. With the help of YouTube and DIY videos, along with some citizens in Normal, including Dottie and Henry, I had taken down all the walls and replaced them with the farmer-style shiplap, added chippy furniture I'd gotten from the Thrifty Nickle, a local thrift shop, and made it the cutest thing you'd ever seen.

I'd even strung twinkling lights around the bedroom to make it girly and romantic so that I didn't miss my bedroom in my Manhattan apartment or Hamptons mansion.

Fifi, geesh, she fit right in with my feminine décor. She loved her fluffy bed, and even though she loved to run around the campground and get her pure, white-as-snow poodle curls all dingy and dirty, she loved going to the Smelly Dog Groomer to have a spa day.

"Hey there." My voice took on a baby-talk tone like it always did when I greeted her.

She was so loyal. Every time I opened the door, she was there, wagging her tail, dancing around on her little feet, her nails ticking against the wood floor.

"It looks like you ate everything." I looked over at her bowl where not even a morsel of kibble was left. "Are you ready to go hike it off?"

I swear she knew what I was saying. She danced around and around next to the small basket near the door next to the passenger captain chair where I kept her leash. If we were going to the office, I generally never put a leash on her. But hiking in the woods was different. Especially during this season.

It was mating season for all the animals in the forest, and they would snatch up my little girl for a treat if I weren't careful.

"Okay." I laughed, trying to calm her down after she started to whine and scratch on the door. "Hold your horses. I've got to get my boots on."

She sat down on my command, watching me with her sweet little round dark eyes as I put my shoes on. When I grabbed the walking stick, she lost her marbles.

Barking and carrying on, dancing and twirling, Fifi was a sight. I just loved her.

She darted out of the door quicker than I could get down the little metal steps. My arm jerked as she extended the fully retractable leash as far as she could go. Thank goodness for harnesses because she'd choke herself if the leash was clipped on her collar.

"Fine, we can go on that trail," I told her once I caught up to her.

There were several trails around the campground. Each trail had a marking from the Wildlife and Forestry Association with the length of the trail, where they could go on the trail, and the level of difficulty.

As the owner of the campground, I'd done all the trails and knew them like the back of my hand. Of course Fifi would pick Red Fox Trail, which was aptly named because there were a lot of red foxes around these parts, and they seemed to love that trail in the park. If she weren't on her leash, I'd have to have told her no and picked another trail. The stench I smelled every time the wind decided to change was probably due to one of those red foxes.

The trail was one of the longer trails, mainly winding downhill. It was going back up that was the killer on my thighs. I'd locked Fifi's retractable leash into place so she couldn't go off the trail too much. She darted from one new sniff to the next. Every few feet she'd stop and try to tinkle. Though nothing was coming out, I did take each time to get a smell of anything foul or dead. If I did find something, though I wasn't responsible for it, I'd still have it cleaned up so the guests at Happy Trails didn't have to wait for it to decompose and the odor to go away.

The sound of someone whistling brought a smile to my face. When Fifi stopped to pee for the umpteenth time, I could hear the distant trickle of water. I knew we were getting closer and closer to the treasure at the end of Red Fox Trail.

The river and the waterfall.

It was a very popular destination, with other trails in and around the park that led there.

Fifi must've heard the whistling. Her little body got antsy, and she started to whine as she continued to pull me to go faster and faster.

"Okay. I'll let you off right here," I told her since she and I both knew who was doing the happy whistles.

Fifi darted off down the trail with me jogging behind her, my stick held up in the air.

"Hey there, sweet girl." I heard Skip Toliver greet Fifi before I'd seen him. "Where is your mama?"

"Right here." My chest heaved up and down from being so out of shape and chasing after her. "Thank goodness the weather is good so I can get back to hiking and getting in shape."

Who was I kidding? I always said I was going to get in shape by enjoying all of the outdoor activities and even taking Jazzercise from Queenie, but at the end of a long day, it never failed. Hank and I would grab something to eat and binge-watch something on TV, or he'd watch something he liked while I read.

"Business has started to pick up." Skip was crouched down petting Fifi. He nodded and pointed to the empty racks of canoes. "I've got a lot of canoers out and a few white-water rafters on a tour."

Skip Toliver had opened up his canoe and white-water rafting business a couple of seasons ago during the drought, which would be the worst time to open a water business in the park. But somehow he'd stayed afloat and made it through. I made sure I told all the guests at Happy Trails to go see him and gave them his business card.

"I'm so glad everything is great." I looked out at the river. I closed my eyes and let the sound of the rushing water soothe me.

"You two just out for a hike?" he asked and continued to pet Fifi. She'd let him as long as he'd do it too.

"Actually, Fifi needed some outside time to wear her out because I have a lot of guests coming this weekend and need to get paperwork done and the bungalows ready. I'm hoping she'll peter out and sleep the rest of the day." I snapped my fingers for her to leave him alone.

Fifi had actually been a show dog before I'd babysat her for her real owner. I'd allowed Fifi to have full run of the campground while she was in my care, and she ended up taking full advantage of her freedom and discovered Rosco, a bulldog who'd never been neutered. Nine weeks later, along came a few little puppies and the end of Fifi's show dog career. Since she was no longer a moneymaker for her previous owner, I took her and her puppies.

All the puppies were given to a good home, but Fifi still loved Rosco.

"Have you smelled any dead animals around here?" I asked.

"Nothing. Just me and the great outdoors." Skip stood back up and stretched his arms, taking a big, deep breath of fresh air. "'Tis the season."

"Yeah. There's a really foul odor up near the campground, so I thought I would hike a few of the trails to see if I could find the source." I shrugged.

"If you see anyone from the Sierra Club on a trail, tell them their rep never showed up with the new tour schedule." Skip seemed a bit irked.

"You aren't talking about Yaley Woodard, are you?" I questioned.

"Ahh…" He groaned and moved toward the little shack he'd erected for himself for quick cover from the elements. He grabbed something off the wood shelf and brought it over to me. "Is that her?"

I took the brochure with the stapled business card and read her name.

"It sure is." My brows furrowed. "She's missing."

"Missing?" Skip was the type of guy who probably never watched the news. It was probably safe to say that he didn't even own a television.

"Yeah. Apparently, she went to lunch the other day and never came back." I shook the brochure. "Can I keep this?"

"Yeah. I've gotta go." He grabbed his backpack. "I was expecting some of their tours today, and now I have no idea what's going on. I better go call them. See you later, Fifi," he called out on his way over to the canoe that was already in the water and tied up to a tree.

Fifi stood at the water's edge, watching Skip paddle off to wherever he was going. I waved bye.

"I guess we better hit it." I clicked my tongue to get Fifi's attention for her to come to me so I could clip the leash back on her harness.

The closer we got up the hill to the campground, the more whiffs of the rotting smell I would get.

I unclipped Fifi at the top of the trail and let her dart toward the office while I followed closely behind.

Dottie Swaggert was sitting behind her desk. This time she was dressed for the day, and her hair was free of pink sponge curlers.

"Where have you been, baby?" Dottie, too, had that baby voice when she spoke to Fifi. She unscrewed the lid off the jar of dog treats she kept on her desk and handed one to Fifi.

Happy as could be, Fifi ran to the dog bed next to my desk with the treat in her tiny little mouth.

"We hiked Red Fox Trail." I headed to the minifridge and took out a bottle of water. "I'm so out of shape." I walked over to her desk and tossed the brochure on it.

"What's this?" She picked it up.

"A Sierra Club brochure with Yaley Woodard's business card attached," I said between gulps of water. "Skip told me Yaley was supposed to have come to his business with a list of tours they booked, and she never showed." I downed what was left in the water bottle and tossed it into the trash. "I told him she went missing a few days ago."

"No one tried to contact him?" Dottie questioned.

"You'd think they'd go through her client list and send someone out to check on them until she turns up." I shook my head and went back to my desk to see what messages Dottie had taken for me. "I also asked him if he'd smelled anything dead. Of course he hadn't, and I didn't see or smell anything either, but as soon as we got back to the opening of the trail, I smelled it again. We've got to find that dead animal."

I glanced over to see what all the noise Dottie was making was about. She was shuffling through her top desk drawer with a determined look on her face.

"Ah-ha!" She held up a box of matches with a big ole smile on her face. "I've got an idea."

"Does your idea have to do with smoking?" I guessed.

"With smoke." Her eyes grew. "Come on out here. I'm gonna show you an old hunter's trick."

"I can't wait to see this," I muttered and put the stack of messages back down on my desk.

We walked out of the office, and sure enough, that smell had wafted past us.

"Watch this." Dottie struck the match. The smell of sulfur filled around us as the flame exploded from the small stick.

Dottie held it up in the air. The light breeze sent the smoke of the match to the left before blowing it out.

"Did you smell the dead animal?" she asked as she took out another match.

"No." I took a couple of whiffs. "Oh gosh." I fanned my hand in front of my nose. "I do now."

Dottie quickly lit the next match, and the smoke blew the other way.

"Follow the smoke," she said.

With a pinched nose, we followed it, and it led us right to our dumpster.

"Oh my gosh." I couldn't stop laughing. "It's our dumpster. Didn't they come and empty it this week?"

"They did, but we've got to get Henry to clean it with bleach and water." Dottie waved her hand in front of her face. "Or better yet, get a new one."

"Gross." I took a deep breath through my mouth and gripped the handle of the small opening to peek inside just in case I could see exactly what the stink was. "Dottie," I gulped when I looked inside and saw a pair of shoes attached to some legs. "We don't need to call the garbage company. We need to call the police."

CHAPTER THREE

"Well, praise the Lord this happened before the new guests arrived." Smoke billowed out of Dottie's mouth, and she raised her cigaretted hand to the sky as if she was praising the Lord.

I was fairly certain Dottie Swaggert had never stepped foot in the Normal Baptist Church. But who was I to judge. I went on Sundays… well, most Sundays, anyway.

"Mmhhh," I ho-hummed and gnawed on the inside of my cheek as I watched Jerry Truman, the sheriff of Normal, jump right on in the dumpster.

"Looky there." Dottie nudged me with her elbow. "He found something." Dottie was giving the play-by-play as Jerry summoned over a deputy. "I wish I could read lips," Dottie muttered and took a drag.

"Me too." My head was filled with thoughts on who those shoes belonged to. After I'd taken a second look in the dumpster before Jerry got there, I noticed the black low-heeled shoes were a woman's shoe. Dare I say it, my creative mind filled with the photo of Yaley Woodard's missing person flyer.

"He must've told him to call in backup because he's gone over there on his phone." Dottie was now telling me the exact steps the deputy had taken, but I was more focused on Jerry.

He was straddled on the outside ledge of the dumpster, taking photos with his phone. He turned around, and our eyes caught.

"Mae, do you have a big stick or see one around?" he hollered over.

"Yeah!" I hurried back inside the office and grabbed my walking stick. I rushed back out the door to give it to him. "Do you know who it is?"

"No. I think it's a woman, but her body is buried by trash. I don't want to disturb the scene, but I see a purse over in the corner." He took my stick and leaned into the dumpster, grunting and groaning as he tried to reach the purse. "Got it," he gasped and tugged the stick up from the garbage can.

He steadied the purse that was dangling from the stick and slowly got down from the dumpster. The deputy had retrieved evidence bags from his car. He opened one of the bags wide and let Jerry slip the purse inside.

"Here you go." Jerry offered me the stick back.

"No, thank you." There was no way I wanted it back, but it was a great walking stick.

Jerry shrugged and laid the stick on the ground. He plucked a couple of blue gloves from his sheriff's jacket and slipped them over his hands before he dug into the evidence bag and opened the purse.

He took out the wallet inside and opened it.

"Yaley Woodard." His words pierced my heart. "Now, I'm not sure that's her in there, but this is her wallet." His dark eyes looked at me. There was a fear deep inside of them that shook me to my core. "I had a call put in for Hank to meet me out here."

"You think…" I gulped knowing they only called Hank for one reason and one reason only. "Murdered?" I could barely get the word out of my mouth.

Before he could answer, the sound of tires driving over the gravel and grit spitting up underneath them forced our attention away from the purse. A big black sedan was speeding up the campground entrance. Hank was at the wheel.

His green eyes were fixed on the dumpster. The wheels of the car tires came to a screeching halt, and Hank shoved the gearshift into Park.

Hank and Chester, his dog, got out of the car and walked right over to me. He had on his blue suit and his wayfarer sunglasses. His black hair was neatly combed and had just the right amount of hair gel to keep it in place for the day. Normally, I'd be swooning over the cologne he was wearing, but it was no match for the stench coming from the body inside the dumpster.

"Are you okay?" he asked and smoothly pulled his sunglasses off his face, exposing the concerned look deep within his green eyes.

"Forget her." Dottie pushed her way into our conversation. "What about me? I've been smelling that for the better part of two days."

"Two days?" Hank suddenly took a vested interest in Dottie. "Are you sure?"

"Do you smell that?" she asked with sarcasm. "When you have that god-awful scent around, you know when it started. Two days." She stuck up two fingers in the air.

"If you two are okay, I'm going to go talk to Jerry." Hank looked between me and Dottie to make sure we were fine. His interaction with us was more on a personal level than his professional detective attitude, which I knew would turn on pretty quickly.

"Come on, Chester." Dottie patted her leg and took him inside the office while I stood there and watched Hank.

No sooner did Dottie shut the door than the sound of more tires spitting up gravel could be heard coming up the entrance of the campground.

Hank, Jerry, Henry, the deputy, and I turned all of our attention to see who was going to pop up around the curve of the road.

The old van was one I knew well. It was Betts Hager, and if I was a bettin' woman, I'd put a thousand dollars on her van having a couple more people in there. And I was right.

I tried not to look at Hank, but it was too late. His long, hard stare and the big, deep breath he took told me he wasn't happy the Laundry Club ladies had shown up, though he shouldn't have been surprised.

Betts Hager, Abby Fawn, Queenie French, Dottie Swaggert, and I had become fast friends. If it weren't for their friendship and support, I probably would've sold the campground and gone back to being a flight attendant.

Betts owned the Laundry Club, the local laundromat. But the Laundry Club was more than just a laundromat. Betts had made it a nice hangout spot for tourists and campers to get their laundry cleaned. She offered a family-room-style television area, a game area, a small library, and a coffee bar. It was a place where we all liked to gather for our monthly book club and other things… like trying our own hand at amateur sleuthing, which was probably why Hank had let out such a big sigh.

"I finished laundering your bed linens for the bungalows, so we gals thought we'd just bring them out to you." Betts nervously pushed her long, wavy brown hair behind her shoulder. Though she was trying to hide her eyes behind her bangs, her cracking voice told me she was lying.

Lying was not Betts's strong suit. Maybe it was because she was the ex-wife of a preacher, or that she was so involved in the church that her moral compass made it hard, even in a small white lie.

"And you had to bring everyone along with you?" Hank nodded to Abby and Queenie, both of whom were carrying some of my bed linens. "Or was it the police scanner that had you out here in a flash?"

Abby and Queenie knew to keep their mouths shut. Out of habit, Abby balanced the bedding in one hand while she scrolled her phone with the other. She was a whiz in the social media department, plus our local librarian.

Queenie busied her nervous feet with some kick-ball-change moves she taught in Jazzercise.

"That too." Betts nibbled on her bottom lip and turned directly to me. "Where would you like them?"

"I guess we can just put those inside." I nodded for the girls to follow me.

All three of them hurried behind me on my heels. They put the linens on the desk before they turned all their attention to me.

"What happened?" Queenie adjusted the terry cloth headband up on her short blond head of hair. She twisted the fanny pack strapped around her waist to the front of her body and unzipped the pouch, taking out her lipstick.

"Don't leave out any details." Abby grabbed the dry-erase marker off Dottie's desk and headed to the dry-erase board. "Do we need any of this on here?" She waved the eraser in front of all the things Dottie had written on the board earlier this morning.

Dottie's mouth opened, then closed, and then opened again like she was going to protest but turned to me for some guidance.

"Whoa." I walked over to Abby and took the eraser from her. "One second here."

Betts was quiet.

"What's wrong, Betts?" I asked. Everyone looked at her.

"I'm not good at lying. How can I help solve cases if I can't even keep an even skin color while telling a simple lie?" Then she started to justify things. "Yes. We heard on the scanner at the Laundry Club about the body. Yes. Your dry cleaning was finished, so I simply suggested to the girls that we bring it to you."

"It's fine." I tried to comfort her, but she was just too good-hearted to bring into the fold of telling even the smallest of tales. "But you bring more to the table than you know. Like your van." I looked at all the gals to give Betts some encouragement. "If it weren't for your side hustle of housecleaning or even your van to get us all from point A to point B, sometimes the little cases we've looked into wouldn't've been solved."

I used air quotes around "cases we've looked into." On the down low, that completely meant that we'd stuck our noses in places and people's business where we had no right to stick our noses. Granted, most of the time we were collectively trying to get some answers to aid Hank in his investigations, so I'm sure when he saw Betts's van, he knew deep down we were going to discuss this body.

"For the bigger picture," I turned my attention to Abby, who had already written "Jane Doe" on part of the dry-erase board with various lines coming out from the name, "our Jane Doe is probably Yaley Woodard, and we don't even know how she died. Or even if there is a case."

"So," Dottie butted in, "are you trying to tell me that Yaley decided to come on out here to Happy Trails, climb into that dumpster herself, and then couldn't get out? Her death was accidental? Because I ain't gonna lie. I seen Joel Grassle myself drive right up to that dumpster the other afternoon and dump in something that looked like a tarp." She wrung her hands. "I'm nervous as a chicken covered in mustard." She reached for her cigarette case.

"Are you sure you saw him?" I questioned. Though I'd only known Joel for a couple of years, I never pictured him killing anyone. He was the complete opposite. The Joel I knew was always helping people, including me.

When Bobby Ray showed up on the doorstep of my RV one Christmas, he came with nothing but the clothes on his back. He needed a place to live and a job. I provided him with one of the bungalows, wood for the fire, and a mini heater, as well as food. But it was Joel who offered Bobby Ray the mechanics job down at Grassle's Garage in downtown Normal.

"Well, hell's bells." Dottie looked at me. "Are you saying I've got bad eyes? I've known Joel all his living life. I'd know him if I saw him in the daylight and the darkness. It was Joel Grassle!"

"What about Joel?" Hank opened the door just as Dottie was hosting her own hissy fit.

Dottie swallowed hard. Her eyes darted between me and Hank.

"Well?" Hank asked with his brows lifted. "I'm waiting to hear what you ladies think. I can see you've already started your theories."

His eyes moved past me and focused on the whiteboard where Abby had written "Jane Doe."

"It's Yaley, isn't it?" I asked, even though I knew deep down, it was her.

"It is, and if you ladies will excuse me, I'd like to ask Dottie and Mae a few questions." He wasn't really asking for the other girls' permission.

"We don't mind." Queenie propped herself up on the edge of Dottie's desk. "Do we?" she asked Betts and Abby. Both shook their heads, and none of them budged.

Hank sucked in a deep breath. He held it for a couple of seconds before he finally let it out in one long and steady stream.

"Fine. I'll take them outside." He turned and fully expected me and Dottie to follow him, which we did.

Once outside, I noticed Colonel Holz had pulled the coroner hearse right up to the dumpster. His gurney was already locked into position, and he was in the dumpster with Jerry.

"As you are aware, the body in the dumpster does match the identification Jerry found in the wallet from the purse he retrieved from the dumpster." Hank had put on his professional face and was very precise in the words he used. "Do you two feel up to answering a few questions?"

"Sure do. I'm fine." Dottie unsnapped the top of the cigarette holder and tapped out one of her smokes.

"I'm good too." I tried to smile at Hank, but he didn't bother looking at me. He took his notepad out of his suit coat pocket and flipped it open. He reached inside his coat and retrieved a pen. "Dottie, you mentioned you smelled the stench a couple of days ago." He looked at her for confirmation. "If that's the case, she's been here a couple of days." He looked up at the security camera I had on the office gutter. "Did you see anyone put anything out of the ordinary in the dumpster?"

"What do you mean by 'out of the ordinary?'" Her eyes narrowed, but I could tell she was contemplating whether or not to tell him she saw Joel Grassle pull up and put something that resembled a tarp in it.

"Other than you, Henry, Mae," he said with a bite of frustration. "Your guests." He gestured around the campground. "People who live here like me, Ty, Bobby Ray…" His voice trailed off as he looked at her as though he were trying to see if she understood the question.

"Hmmmm." She put her cigarette up to her mouth and took a nice long drag.

"She did." As much as I wanted to keep my mouth shut because Joel was my friend, it was news too big to keep from Hank. He could at least talk to Joel.

"Mae!" Dottie huffed and gave me the stink eye. "I was trying to figure out how to tell him."

"Tell me what? Or tell me who?" Hank asked, his chin falling to his chest, his eyes looking at her under his brows.

"Joel Grassle." She took another puff and then threw the cigarette on the ground, snuffing it out with the toe of her shoe before she bent over to pick it up. "The other day, I was watching *Little House on the Prairie*, you know the one where Ma and Pa renewed their wedding vows."

"Dottie, stick to Joel." Hank appeared to have his fill of Dottie already, and the questioning was just getting started.

"Anyways, I heard some noise. By instinct and living right here at the front of the campground, I looked out my window and saw Joel's pickup pull up to the dumpster. He was tossing some stuff in it, and then I saw him pick up a tarp." She crossed her arms. "That's all I know."

"Did he see you?" Hank asked.

"I don't know. I didn't open the door. It was my lunch hour, and I wasn't going to go out there and see why he thought he could just dump his crap in our dumpster." Dottie turned to me. "Ain't that illegal to use someone else's dumpster?"

"I-I have no clue," I stammered, still trying to wrap my head around the thought that Joel killed Yaley.

"Do you know anything about Joel and Yaley?" Hank asked us.

"I had heard they were dating from Violet, but that's it. Bobby Ray hasn't said anything to me." I left out the gossip I'd gotten from Alvin Deters that Joel had mentioned it, making me feel like it was casual. "Joel certainly didn't say anything."

"What 'bout the brochure?" Dottie nudged me then nodded for me to tell Hank.

"What brochure?" Hank looked at me.

"Fifi and I went on a hike down Red Fox Trail. I, too, had smelled the stench and thought it was some sort of dead animal since it's mating season, and you know how they hunt. I talked to Skip Toliver. He asked if I'd seen Yaley on any of the trails because he figured she was lost. Or maybe he was joking. I'm not sure, either way." I looked over when I heard some noise coming from the dumpster. I continued, "He said Yaley was supposed to drop off the new tour schedule. When I told him that she'd been missing for a couple of days, he took off downriver in his canoe. He relies on the tour companies for his income."

I kept my eye on the dumpster. Jerry and Colonel were both bent over. They were opposite each other about five or six feet apart. They both stood up at the same time. My heart sank when I realized they were hoisting Yaley's body out of the dumpster. Jerry had the body under the armpits, her limp arms dangling while Colonel had her legs. With the help of the deputy, they safely and gingerly took her out of the dumpster and placed her on the gurney.

I wanted to look away, but I couldn't.

"Can I go see her?" I knew it was an unusual question, but I wanted so bad to send some sort of prayer to her. It was terrible how she was discarded like she was trash.

"Sure." Hank looked at Dottie.

"Oh, heck no." She took out another cigarette. "I'm fine right here, keeping my distance."

"Are you sure you're okay?" Hank reached over and touched me.

"I'm fine. I just hate that she was put in a dumpster." I shook my head and tried to make sense of it all.

"You wouldn't believe how many homicides are found in dumpsters across the United States, but generally, the killer knows when the garbage truck is coming, so the body won't decompose." He and I stopped at the gurney.

Colonel was writing down the report and making notes on the clipboard while Jerry was still dumpster diving for clues. The other deputy was searching the area around the dumpster for any other clues.

"I'd like to get a copy of your security camera film," Hank noted.

"Unfortunately, Joel was here a few days ago, and the film tapes over itself every forty-eight hours." I knew my information was going to burst his bubble, but I was too focused on Yaley as she laid on the gurney.

The image of the smiling face I'd seen earlier on the flyer was still very much burned in my memory, and it didn't match the young woman I was staring at.

"Where's her heart necklace?" I noticed the adorable heart-shaped necklace she'd worn in the photo wasn't around her neck. "The flyer specifically said she always wore the heart necklace in the photo."

"Are you sure?" Hank asked, using his pen to move some of the collar from her neck. "Geez, strangled." Hank looked up at Colonel.

"It appears so, but I won't be able to determine it was death by strangulation until I do a complete autopsy." Colonel and Hank talked death shop while I recalled the flyer.

"I'm telling you, the flyer said she never took off the necklace." I pleaded with Hank to check into it. I held up a finger for him to hold on. "I have the flyer."

I hurried back inside the office to retrieve the flyer from my cross-body. Betts, Queenie, and Abby couldn't get away from the window fast enough.

"What's going on?" Abby asked. The three of them stood looking at me while I rummaged through my bag.

"It's Yaley, and she isn't wearing her heart necklace." I unfolded the flyer and showed it to them. "I told Hank she always wore the necklace, and it says so right here."

"Where you going with that?" Queenie shuffle-ball-changed in front of me.

"I'm giving it to Hank." I tried to move past her, but she shuffled that way.

"No. You make a copy and give him the copy." Queenie put her hands on her hips and gave me the side-eye.

I turned around to look at Betts and Abby. Abby had already erased the entire list of chores I needed to do for Happy Trails, and they'd already started the murder investigation grid with the victim, suspects, and motive blocks. She was writing under Yaley's name how the heart necklace was missing.

My heart dropped down into my toes when the only name I saw on the suspect list was Joel Grassle.

"Give Hank the photocopy." Betts walked over and took the flyer by pinching the corner and holding it up to take over to the copier.

"Fine." I took the copied flyer and headed back out to give it to Hank. Dottie was still smoking, waiting for Hank to ask her some more questions. "Here you go. See. If you look closely, there are diamonds around the circumference."

I pointed to the necklace and then pointed to where the information said a possible identifier was her necklace.

"Are you sure those are diamonds?" Hank asked.

"Seriously, Hank?" I drew back, almost offended. "If any girl would know a diamond, no matter how small these are, I'm the girl."

He smiled and shook his head. He brought the paper up to his face and looked a little closer.

"Jerry," Hank yelled over the top of the dumpster. "We need to take everything out of the dumpster. We need to find a heart-shaped necklace."

"It has small diamonds around it," I added.

Jerry's head popped up over the top of the dumpster. He called the deputy over to him and told him to call in a few more deputies so that they could take the contents out of the dumpster in a very meticulous order.

"I don't have any funerals down at the funeral home, so I can get you a preliminary report by the end of the day and probably a full autopsy by the end of the week." Colonel handed his clipboard and pen to Jerry, who signed it.

"Don't do anything until Agnes calls the next of kin," Jerry told the coroner.

"Oh, I won't. I've known this family for a long time." Colonel shook his head, his mouth turned down in a frown. "I sure do hate that this happened to such a sweet gal."

"We are going to have to do thorough checks in and around the campground. We are going to position a park ranger at the front of the entrance so they can vet who comes and goes." Jerry was spouting off his protocol, which meant I was going to be shut down for business until they had scoured every blade of grass, piece of gravel, and inch of the tree line.

"Jerry," I gasped. "How long will that take? I've got new guests arriving in the next few days, and it's my busy season."

Not that I was minimalizing Yaley's poor demise, but it would be my demise if I couldn't pay my bills. It wasn't like we functioned in the black all year long. I made most of the money during the late spring and summer months, which had to be budgeted for the low seasons, like winter when it snowed.

"It's going to be a couple of days." Hank didn't make me feel any better as he waved Dottie over. "Dottie, have you ever given Joel permission to use the dumpster?"

Oh, good question, I thought and looked at her.

"You know, after all these years, I might've, I might not've." She flicked the ash from her cigarette. "I tell people they can do things all the time without checking with Mae, and who knows what I said to people in the community before Mae came along."

Hank had his notebook open and was writing down everything Dottie was saying. Before he could even look up, Violet Rhinehammer and her cameraman were barreling up the drive.

"I need someone from the ranger department here now!" Jerry yelled to the poor deputy who was trying to do all the other tasks Jerry had spouted out for him.

Jerry hurried over to the media van and stuck his hand out. He gestured for them to roll the window down.

Hank put his attention back on his notebook and continued to question Dottie.

"Did you see or hear anything else that night?" he asked her.

"Hank, I can't recall what I heard this morning, much less a couple nights ago." Dottie Swaggert lied right there in front of me.

She was better with gossip and happenings with everyone around Normal. She was like a walking, talking National Enquirer for Normal, Kentucky.

"How many people were staying in the campground that night?" Hank moved his question to me.

"It was Monday. I do recall that because I was watching my show. I work all day in the office on Monday, and I was eatin' lunch. *Little House* was on." Dottie gave a hard nod, at least giving Hank something to hang his hat on. "Sunday is the last day on the weekly contracts, and we didn't take any guest contracts this week so Mae could get the bungalows ready and restocked, so we don't have to shut down for the rest of the season. I'm for sure it was Monday."

Hank continued to take notes. I stayed silent so I could hear exactly where Dottie was going with this.

"I'm figuring the only people left living here are you, Mae, Bobby Ray, me, Ty, and Henry." Dottie counted on her fingers as she spouted off the names. "Six people."

"It's pretty early today. Has anyone left this morning?" he asked.

"I'd just got back from a hike, so I didn't see anyone come or go." I looked over at Dottie. "You?"

"You can take a look down yonder and see if anyone's cars are gone from their campers." Dottie wasn't trying to be funny, but she was funny by nature.

Hank let out another long sigh. It was more than I'd ever heard him release, and I knew his fuse was getting cut short.

"I know Henry is here. That's it. As for Bobby Ray, I'm not sure. I did see Ty at the diner this morning." I was going to suggest that I could call Bobby Ray but was interrupted.

"Sir?" the deputy called to Hank. "I think you should see this."

Jerry was still talking to Violet, who appeared to have worked her charm. In the driver's-side seat, the cameraman had hoisted the camera onto his shoulder, and Violet had the microphone stuck outside the window.

"Mae, you and Dottie can go on in the office now," Hank said. "I'll come find you when we are done here. But I'm telling you, the campground will not be open to guests until we feel we've gotten all the evidence collected."

Hank headed on over to the dumpster, where the deputy had called him to.

"I see that look in your eye." Dottie walked sideways and eyeballed me. "What is it you're thinkin'?"

"I'm thinking that the Laundry Club ladies are going to have to look into things on their own." I pushed the sleeves of my sweatshirt up to my elbows. "I know Joel Grassle didn't kill anyone. If we don't find the real killer and soon, then we can kiss the future of this campground goodbye. Because we have to have guests in order to stay afloat. It's Thursday, which means we've got until Sunday to catch this killer."

CHAPTER FOUR

The Laundry Club gals had decided to take the investigation over to the lake. It was one area Hank and Jerry hadn't roped off with yellow tape. It also gave me time to take Fifi for a walk and put her in the camper while I got the notebook.

"You be a good girl." I fluffed up her dog bed and made sure she had some water. She'd already eaten her breakfast, and her belly was full of treats the gals had given her while I was outside being questioned by Hank.

I opened one of the kitchen drawers to grab the notebook the Laundry Club gals and I had used to keep notes on previous crimes we'd stuck our noses into. Granted, we had more theories in there than facts, but some of those led to the arrest of the criminals. This was no different.

Dottie, Betts, Queenie, and Abby had pulled up Adirondack chairs on the pier of the lake. They all faced the front of the campground and the dumpster. Colonel Holz must've gotten the all clear from Hank to take Yaley's body because I noticed he was leaving when I was walking over to the pier.

Queenie reached for the notebook so she could take notes. She looked at Yaley's missing person flyer I had folded up and stuck in there so we had it. I walked over to the little beach next to the pier and dragged a chair over for me.

"Oh no." Abby continued to swipe her phone screen. "Everyone is on social about the murder. Luckily, I don't see anyone tagging Happy Trails. Just the Daniel Boone National Forest."

"Already?" I could feel the despair settling in my gut. I curled my leg up under me. "I thought we would have a couple of days before it was all over. I have to find out who killed her, and in a couple of days, because I'm worried about my guests canceling."

"At least it's the park they are talking about." Queenie did a couple of neck rolls. "That takes up way more than Normal."

"If they do find it's Happy Trails, we could be in trouble. It's our busy time too." There was a look of worry knotted on Dottie's face. She was right. I took whatever extra money we made during the next five months, and we lived on that for the rest of the year, including repairs and upgrades. "What are we going to do?"

"We are going to find out who killed her, and then Hank will take down the tape, remove the ranger from the entrance, and we will be open for business." It seemed like a very practical plan, but practicality was never a strong suit in Normal.

"Two days?" Betts questioned. "How are we going to do that?"

"I would love to help, but I'm scheduled to work at the library for the next week because I'm filling in for vacations." Abby couldn't get her fingernails down into the investigation, but she was very valuable. "I'll do some background checks on Yaley's family, social media, and see if anyone knew her when they come in the library. Idle chitchat." She wiggled her brows.

"Sometimes idle chitchat brings on good gossip that'll take us to a lead." I looked at Queenie. "Are you taking notes?"

"Yeppers." She nodded. "I've got a few Jazzercise classes going on, so I'm limited to what I can do to snoop around, but I do know there are a few ladies from the Sierra Club that do come, so I'll see what they know."

"Perfect. I will go to the Sierra Club to see what they are going to do about the tours around Happy Trails. Maybe I can get someone to talk." I figured that'd be my first stop since it was very important for my business to make sure these tours were being offered to my guests.

"What can I do?" Betts asked.

"I'm not sure." I adjusted myself and tried to think. "What about your Bible-beater group? Anyone there work for the Sierra Club?"

The Sierra Club was a pretty big tour company to work for. There were very few businesses in and around the Daniel Boone National Forest, meaning most worked together or at least knew each other. It was like a big factory in a small town. Every citizen in that small town worked for the factory. It was no different with the various tour businesses here. It just so happened that the Sierra Club was located close to Normal, and that's where a lot of our citizens worked if they didn't own a shop in downtown.

"I have a few stay-at-home moms I can talk to. In fact, we have our weekly Normal Baptist Church Women's Club meeting this week, and I can see if anyone knows anything." Betts shrugged.

"Ask for some prayer requests or somethin'." Dottie lit up a cigarette. "You know they all like to be prayed for over at your joint."

"It's a church, Dottie." Betts let out a long, deep sigh and shook a finger at Dottie. "Maybe you need to be prayed over to stop smoking those."

"Me and you 'bout to have our own come-to-Jesus meetin'," Dottie muttered under her breath. It was as though everyone was on edge, and I needed to keep the peace.

"I can also go see Agnes Swift." I was referring to Hank's grandmother. She worked at the police station and didn't mind sharing things she'd heard about. At least, she didn't mind sharing with me. "The other night Hank and I had gone over to her house for supper, and I told her I'd bring Fifi back to play with Precious."

Precious was one of Fifi's puppies. When I took Fifi over there, it was like she knew she was Precious's mother. It was so sweet how Fifi's instincts had taken over and how she groomed Precious.

"It sounds like we all have something to do." Betts got up. "Did you write it all down, Queenie?"

"Of course I did," Queenie snapped. She must've realized it too. "I'm sorry, Betts. I think we are all a little stressed about it. Let's all take a moment to take a big, deep breath."

She looked around at each one of us.

"Come on. Take a deep breath." Queenie sucked in some air, filled her chest, and rolled her shoulders. "Close your eyes, and let that breath out of your mouth in a slow, steady stream."

I tried to keep the sound of my steady stream silent, but not Dottie. She sounded like she was pushing wind through a fan.

I opened one eye and looked her way. Her eyes were closed, and she was sucking wind. I tried not to laugh, but it fell out of me. The laughter spread amongst the five of us, echoing all over the campground and bouncing off the mountains.

Hank and Jerry looked over at us and probably thought we were nuts, all trying to take big, deep breaths. Still, it helped everyone calm down. We all hugged each other goodbye, and before I knew it, Dottie and I were left standing on the pier.

"You didn't make no mention about Joel Grassle." Dottie pointed out the obvious.

"I didn't want to alarm anyone." I looked out over the lake and the sun's rays falling over the still water. "I thought I'd look into it myself. I don't want anyone in town to think Joel did it, and his business take a hit too." I put my hand over my brows to shield from the sun so I could look in her eyes. "Are you sure it was Joel?"

"I didn't see him, but I knew it was his truck. Well, I heard his truck." Dottie and I both knew Joel's beat-up blue truck. "I've been telling him for years that he needs to fix that dadgum muffler because it sounded like he was about to take off like a rocket or somethin'."

"There is no denying that truck." I took another deep breath like Queenie had us do because, for some reason, it did feel good right about now.

"It's gonna be a hot one today." Dottie put her hands on her hips and looked around. "I guess I can get some of them sheets on the beds in the bungalows if you want to go look around."

"Are you sure?" I asked and fixated my eyes on Bobby Ray's bungalow. His car was gone, and I could use the excuse that I wanted to see him since he did work for Joel down at Grassle's Garage.

"Yep. Don't mind a bit. Especially if it's gonna get this here murder solved, and we can take down all that police tape before our busy season starts." Dottie took a couple of steps back and stumbled.

"Dottie!" I rushed over and grabbed her, steadying her on her feet. "Are you okay? You're a little pale."

"I'm finer than frog's hair." She batted me away. "I didn't eat breakfast yet, and seeing that dead body gave me the willies."

There was no sense in going after her. Dottie was as bullheaded as they came. She, for sure, wasn't going to get checked out even if I asked her to or even offered for the doctor to come here. If she said she was fine, I was going to have to believe her.

CHAPTER FIVE

There wasn't a single cloud in the sky. The sun was bright and really made the mountains in the forest come alive. The various colors of green were painted all over the backdrop, no matter where you looked. It was hard not to feel thankful as the bursts of yellow, purple, red, and white wildflowers popped up in bundles along the country road.

The forest was definitely something to see this time of the year. The wet spring had started to dry up, which gave the extra special drinks of water to the limestone in the Kentucky soil to bring out the vibrant rainbow of colors. They brought happiness and joy into the world where such an unkind deed had happened. And it was hard to wrap my head around Joel Grassle being Hank's number one suspect.

Though Hank didn't say Joel was, I could see that Hank had thought it. Especially with Dottie being able to ID him. Honestly, Joel hadn't been the same since his brother had died. We all had seen the subtle changes in him. He and his brother were close. It was like a piece of him had been buried along with his brother, but I thought he was really coming along.

Grief did strange things to people. I knew that. My grief over my family's death had turned me into someone I didn't recognize when I was muddling through my teenage years. Many times I fought with people I loved, like Mary Elizabeth, my adoptive mother, and maybe there were a few times I had wished she were dead. Granted, I was a teenager, and now I knew that was awful to admit. But maybe Joel and Yaley had an argument. He lost his temper and killed her.

The thought of it just made me sick to my stomach. My car passed through downtown, where I saw a few tourists walking around, and when I passed Grassle's Garage, I saw Joel and Bobby Ray were there.

Instead of stopping and making something up, I drove past and headed toward the business district where the various banks and offices were located. That also included the sheriff's department and The Cookie Crumble. When the bakery came to Normal, there weren't any of the cottage-style shops available to rent, so Christine and her sister Mallory built their own shop. It was a lot more modern than most businesses, but very well received. Plus, I knew Bobby Ray and Joel loved the donuts from there.

The open sign hanging on the window of The Cookie Crumble blinked. I smiled knowing I could get a few donuts for Bobby Ray and Joel to take with me to the garage so they wouldn't think I was doing something out of the ordinary. On many occasions, I'd stop by the garage and always brought some sort of treat with me. The only time I did go empty-handed was when my little car, which I'd bought from Joel when I moved to Normal, needed something.

I smiled at the memory. I'd rolled into town in that beat-up pop-up camper. I was like the eyesore that owned an eyesore. Plus, I had to drive it all over town to get from one place to the other. Finally, I had decided it was too much money for the gas guzzler, and Grassle's Garage offered rental cars and SUV-type cars for people who did want to get around without driving their RV everywhere. He suggested I just buy the small four-door, and he gave me a deal.

Remembering these times with Joel made me question if he really did kill Yaley. But the evidence that Hank and Jerry had collected would tell the true story.

"Did I get the dates wrong?" Christine Watson's eyes grew when she looked up after hearing the bell over the door ding when I walked in.

"Nope. In a couple of days, the recreation room opens. I'm here to get some personal donuts." I almost gave the poor girl a heart attack. Christine and I had a deal where she provided the morning donuts and afternoon cookies for the recreation room.

Of course, it wasn't free. I paid her, but if I wasn't going to have seasonal guests right off the bat, it might be an expense I'd have to cut out. Though I wasn't going to tell her that.

"Oh, I have your favorite maple-glazed Long Johns." She smiled, causing the freckles across her nose to grow wider. Her long brown hair was pulled into a low ponytail at the nape of her neck. She had on an apron with The Cookie Crumble Bakery logo on it.

"What do Bobby Ray and Joel like to get?" I asked.

"Bobby Ray likes the Long Johns like you and Joel." She shook her head. "Oh, Joel. That boy is in love. He was in here on Monday morning picking up some apple strudels for his lady friend."

"Was she with him?" I questioned.

"She stayed in the truck. It was early too." She winked. "I mean really early, like five-thirty-when-I-open early."

"When did you say this was?" I questioned.

"Two…" She hesitated. "No. Three days ago. Because Dawn Gentry had dropped off some fresh milk, and I came in early to meet her. And Dawn had given Joel a quart of milk she had in the truck because it goes so good with the strudel. At least, she and Mary Elizabeth say their bed-and-breakfast clients love the combination."

"Did you see the woman he had in his car?" I asked.

"No. It's still dark that early. Why?" she asked with curiosity.

"I'd heard a rumor he was dating someone and just wanted to know who." I focused my attention on the display case. "I'll take a few of the strudels then."

"And what would you like for yourself?" She plucked a couple of the plastic napkins from the holder and a to-go box.

"I don't think I want anything. My stomach is a little upset this morning." I wondered if I was going to regret getting the strudels and how Joel was going to react to me when I gave them to him. It would be a good opportunity to tell him that I'd heard he'd gotten some a couple of days ago. It would be in front of Bobby Ray, and I knew Bobby Ray wouldn't let Joel do anything to me.

"I hope your stomach feels better." Christine met me over at the register.

I dug my debit card out of my bag and swiped it to finish the sale.

"I'm sure I'll be fine." I looked over her shoulder at the television screen where the interview Violet Rhinehammer had done with Jerry was playing on the television. I gulped. Word was going to get around fast now that it was airing. Clearly, you could see it was Happy Trails, and it didn't help that the cameraman had panned over to Dottie Swaggert smoking her cigarette outside of the office. "Thanks, though."

"Let me know if I can do anything," Christine called out to me when I headed out the door.

I couldn't help but look over at the sheriff's department that was attached to the side of the courthouse. Hank's car was parked in his usual space, so I knew I couldn't stop by just yet to see what Agnes had heard, especially about Joel.

The only way for me to satisfy my itch of curiosity and see if I could somehow throw on my sleuth hat was to go to the source. Grassle Garage, where Joel would welcome these donuts.

Downtown was just a short distance from the business district, and when I pulled in, Joel and Bobby Ray were still hunkered over the engine of a car. Both of them were pointing and discussing. Bobby Ray had always been good with cars when we were growing up. He could get anything with an engine working. He had gone one step further after he realized the car industry was going digital and had continued his education to learn all the nuts and bolts of the electrical equipment being installed in cars.

Both of them looked over their shoulder to see who was driving up. They stood straight up at the same time and wiped their hands down the towels fastened on the pockets of their work jumpsuits.

I reached over, picked up The Cookie Crumble box, and held it up in the air. I was happy to see some smiling faces.

"I saw you two working so hard when I drove past to go to the bakery, I figured I'd stop by on my way back to the campground." I handed the box to Bobby Ray, and he immediately opened it.

"Come on in for a cup of coffee." Joel gestured for me to follow him into the garage.

Just as we got into the office and sat down, a car pulled up to the gas pump, causing the hose to ding the bell located inside of the office, letting Joel and Bobby Ray know there was a customer.

"Eat." Joel put his hand up when Bobby Ray set his donut down on the desk. "I'll go pump and be quick about it."

Grassle's Garage was one of very few left where they pumped their clients' gas. It was so southern gentlemanly of them. He didn't even raise the price of gas because they were the only gas station in Normal. Joel was such a good guy in so many ways, which was why I questioned if he really did kill Yaley.

"How's it going, May-bell-ine?" Bobby Ray asked around a mouthful of maple-glazed Long John.

"Honestly, I stopped by to see if you knew anything about Joel and Yaley." I looked at the pump to make sure Joel wasn't coming back.

He was busy using the window squeegee to clean the windshield of the client. I could see they were having a conversation.

"I think they broke up a few days ago. He said they had an argument and called it off." He shrugged. "I think it was up in the night too. Because he came in here pretty tore up. He even got some car repair orders wrong and changed the oil in one vehicle that needed a tire repair." Bobby Ray shook his head while he washed down the donut with a sip of coffee. "Why you asking?"

Bobby Ray looked past me, causing me to turn around to see what had gotten his attention.

Hank Sharp.

"Oh no." I turned back to Bobby Ray and closed my eyes to try and come up with an excuse to why I'd stopped by when Hank asked me, because he would ask me.

"May-bell-ine, what's going on?" Bobby Ray asked with a tense tone.

"Yaley was found in the dumpster at Happy Trails, dead." I gulped. "In a tarp, and Dottie saw Joel pull up in his truck and throw the tarp in there."

"In his truck. The one that needs a new muffler?" Bobby Ray had a look of disbelief on his face. "That truck was stolen the day he and Yaley broke up. And Joel couldn't kill anyone. This is ridiculous."

"Are you his alibi?" I asked Bobby Ray because this was serious, and Joel was going to need one.

"No. I was off, but—" Bobby Ray stopped talking.

Bobby Ray got up and walked out of the office like he was going to do some wrestling tag team with his buddy.

There was a three-way conversation going on among them after the customer had left, and Hank motioned for me to come out of the office.

"Fancy seeing you here." I offered a smile, though I really wanted to see his eyes underneath his sunglasses. "I just stopped by to—"

"Can I see you over here?" Hank interrupted me and obviously didn't mean it as an option. He took my hand and dragged me to the side of the garage. "What are you doing here?"

"I was dropping off donuts to my brother." I was. It wasn't a lie. He didn't ask me my motive for the stop.

"Don't give me some bull malarkey about donuts. I know you, and I saw your face when I told you the campground was going to have to close until we combed every inch for evidence. And I know you and the women were over in your little huddle by the lake trying to figure out who knew who and what y'all could find out." Hank stood in his cop stance, his head tilted slightly to the right, hiding his accusing eyes under those glasses. "You and your little gang of sleuths running around Normal, trying to find things out, and then reporting what people are gossiping about to me and Jerry wastes our time." He shifted his weight and paused.

I knew this was his little tactic to give me time to jump in and say something. The uncomfortable silence. But I hunkered down and mentally forced myself to stay silent.

"It wastes our time because we are obligated to follow up on every single piece of information that comes in and not do our own investigating. We are a small team." He had a point, but we never took our clues to him unless it seemed really important.

"My truck was stolen. I didn't throw anything or anyone in a dumpster." Joel Grassle stomped over to us. "I didn't kill Yaley. I dropped her off at her home that morning. We were going to meet for lunch by the amphitheater, but I got caught up in the job I was doing and didn't make it."

Hank let out a long, deep sigh, and I could tell he'd yet to tell Joel why he was really there.

"Is this why you wanted me to come to the sheriff's department? Because I won't." Joel seemed very anxious. "Mae, what's that lawyer's name?"

"Hold on here." Hank tried to calm the situation, but there was no calming Joel or Bobby Ray.

Bobby Ray stood behind Joel with his hands fisted then opened them, wiggled his fingers, and bounced on his toes like he was about to be tagged in.

"I only want you to come down to the office so we can get a statement from you. If your truck was stolen, we can find the police report you filled out, and we can also start looking for the real killer." Hank tried to sweeten the pot as if he was trying to pretend he didn't think Joel was the killer, but I could tell by his attitude he still suspected Joel knew something or had more information.

"I didn't fill out a police report. The truck was old, and it had no value. I never take the keys out, and my insurance would go up if I did report it." Joel's answer couldn't have been any more damning than it was.

I dropped my head and closed my eyes.

"Ava Cox," I whispered, letting Hank know that I'd picked helping Joel over keeping my mouth shut by telling Joel Ava's name.

Ava was a lawyer who'd been able to help me out of a few sticky situations when she certainly owed me nothing.

"Oh, Mae." Hank shuffled his foot and took off his glasses. He wanted me to see his eyes. "Please don't do this. This will hurt us. Let me do my job."

"I'm sorry, Hank. I'm not doing anything to hurt us. I simply want the real killer to be found." I could feel the sting of tears starting in my nose and trying to make their way to my eyes. I gulped a few times.

"Joel, I have no option but to bring you down for questioning." Hank pulled a pair of shiny handcuffs out of his pocket. "Joel Grassle, I'm placing you under arrest for the murder of Yaley Woodard." Hank began to read Joel his rights and slipped a cuff on one wrist before he took Joel's arm behind him and cuffed the other.

Bobby Ray and I stood there with our mouths open while Hank put Joel in his car. Hank didn't even look back at me to see my reaction. He put his sunglasses on and drove straight toward the office.

"Call Ava," Bobby Ray demanded. "Mae. Call her."

"I will. I will." I tried to tell him in a calm voice but wondered why Joel didn't seem to put up any sort of argument when Hank arrested him.

On my way back to the car to get my phone, I couldn't help but wonder what the argument Joel and Yaley had was. Where was the truck when it was stolen? There were so many unanswered questions. What if someone knew she and Joel were dating and planned to kill her? They stole Joel's truck then killed her but knew she and Joel were fighting. Who was close enough to know these things about her?

"Hey Ava." I was never sure how Ava Cox was going to respond to me when I called. Though we'd come to terms with our past, we were still on shaky ground.

"Who's in trouble now?" she asked.

"Trouble?" I wanted to lead in with, "How are you doing?" But she was as straightforward as they come.

"I only hear from you when someone is in trouble. I don't have much time to dillydally with you on the phone, so just spit it out, Mae." Ava sounded a little annoyed.

"My friend Joel Grassle from the gas station has been charged with murder." I walked inside of the garage because Bobby Ray was busy fiddling with a customer at the gas pump, and I couldn't hear.

"You mean the body they found in your dumpster?" she asked. "I've been waiting for your call. I figured you knew her."

"I don't know her. I know who she is, but I don't personally know her. My friend Joel was dating her but conveniently—"

"I don't need to hear the situation from you. I need to hear it from him." I could picture her as she talked to me. Her petite body in her perfectly ironed pantsuit with her long black curly hair pulled into a nice knot on her head. Her olive skin was flawless along with her red lipstick. She was so well put together, and she was a dang good lawyer. "Is he at the sheriff's department?"

"He is." I felt a little relief knowing she was at least going to go talk to him. "At first, I wanted the case solved because our busy season starts soon, and if they have the campground roped off for the investigation, then I can't open. But now I'm worried about my friend. I honestly don't think he did it."

"You let me come to those conclusions, and I'll let you know what I decide to do. I'm on my way." She hung up the phone without saying goodbye.

It was fine with me. I didn't need bedside manners. I wanted someone who was going to get the job done.

CHAPTER SIX

B obby Ray was going to do business as usual because he honestly
thought Joel would be back any minute. I didn't have the heart to
tell him how I knew Hank would enforce the twenty-four-hour hold
unless Ava did some fast-talking to get Joel out. Even with that, his
bond would be set so high, there's no way he'd be getting out anytime
soon.

Instead of driving down to the Laundry Club or even out to the
Sierra Club, I walked down to the Normal Public Library to see Abby.
She was always pretty quick with her part of sleuthing, and I needed the
fresh air to clear out all the crazy notions swirling around in that frizzy
head of mine.

The sliding doors opened right into the heart of the library's big
roomy entrance. Abby liked to have book signings there, though those
were very few and far between, as well as any local events. Sometimes
the local government used the conference room in the small library to
hold meetings.

There was an iron rack with various tourist postcards for things to
do around Normal for tourists to take. Today of all days, the Sierra
Club brochure popped out at me. I plucked it off the rack and opened
it, noticing it was last season's schedule. I stuck it in my pocket after I

noticed their office address on the back where tourists needed to go to sign up for one of their tours.

The library was rarely busy, and it was no different today. I could hear Abby talking. When I followed the voice, it got louder, and I saw she was in her office on the phone. There was a stack of books on her desk. She looked up, the phone cradled between her shoulder and ear. An open book occupied her hands. She used the book to wave me in.

"That's great. I can donate these then. Talk to you soon." Abby hung up the phone. "Good news." She placed her hand on the stack of books. "These can go down to the Laundry Club because we took them out of circulation."

"Betts will love that. I think she's tired of looking at the same ones there now." I loved how Abby would recycle the books to fill the small library shelf Betts kept for her customers at the laundromat and didn't throw them away. I opened The Cookie Crumble box with the strudels and set it on the desk.

"As you can see, we are swamped," Abby joked. "So I've had a bit of time to do a little digging around." She pulled some printed papers from the printer behind her desk. "Yaley Woodard is not from here. She and her brother actually moved here a few years ago. He invested in some rental cabins and owns Lost in the Woods Rental, and she works for the Sierra Club. She used to funnel all the calls for cabin rentals to her brother, but other realtors and VRBO—"

I stopped her.

"VRBO?" I questioned. What in the heck she was talking about? In reality, Abby and I weren't too far off in age, but her lingo and my lingo were worlds apart.

"Vacation rental by owner. It's like Airbnb." She shrugged and took one of the strudels out of the box.

"So you're telling me that she got a job at the Sierra Club where she not only books tours but vacation homes?" That got my attention. "Why aren't I using them?"

"Because you have me, and I'm doing all your social media, and I keep you booked." Abby smiled.

Without Abby and her skills with hashtags and online practices, my campground wouldn't have the business it had. From the beginning, she was great about getting the word out about how the campground was new and improved. She really sold those bungalows to people based on romance and a girl-getaway destination.

"Maybe one of the angry realtors killed her?" I dug down into my hobo bag and got the notebook out. During an investigation, I always kept the notebook with me.

"Maybe." She shrugged. "But I also know that she and her brother didn't get along all that well because I put a call into one of the realtors mentioned in the article."

"There was an article?" I really wanted to know where the article was from and how long ago. "Do you have it?"

"Right here." Abby thumbed through the papers and handed me one. "I printed off all I could find. Apparently, the realtors were going to file a suit against the Sierra Club for some sort of breach to their agreement contract, plus bad business of only funneling tourists to Lost in the Woods. That's when Yaley got demoted and put on tours, which supposedly is the worst job out there."

"So she's not as squeaky-clean as everyone has made her out to be." I was looking over the article and realizing Yaley had a very big past, and it was something I was going to look into.

"She did have a few enemies. You can put these in the notebook so we can go over them tonight at the Laundry Club." Abby handed the rest of the papers to me.

"Tonight?" I asked, and my heart fell into my toes.

"Yeah. Betts, Queenie, and I had thought we'd all get together tonight to go over what we found…" She looked up at me and stopped talking. "What's wrong?"

"I think Hank and I are…" I tried really hard to gulp back the word without crying. But the waterworks turned on.

"You're what?" she asked but quickly rushed around the desk when she saw I was getting a little emotional. "Oh no." She wrapped her arms around me and snuggled me. "Is it because of this?"

I nodded, feeling my tears being wiped down her button-down shirt with the library logo on it.

"This is not worth it, Mae." Abby's words filled my head. "You and Hank have something special. He only wants you to stay safe."

"I can't morally let someone that didn't kill Yaley go to jail." I pulled back and wiped my hand down my face to remove the tears then swiped my finger under my eyes to catch any more falling. I handed the notebook to her. "We need to take notes and maybe talk about Hank later."

The sudden rush of needing to write down what Bobby Ray had told me and what Abby had found out overcame me. Hank and I would be okay. We had to be. I had to believe we would so I could move forward.

Abby took the notebook and went back to sitting at her desk, where she opened to the page and got her pen ready.

I stood up and paced back and forth in the office so my head would remain clear from any thoughts of Hank.

"I went to The Cookie Crumble to get donuts so I could stop by the garage and ask some questions. Christine told me she saw Joel and Yaley in the truck..." My voice trailed off. "Oh my gosh. Who else saw Joel and Yaley in the truck?"

"What?" Abby stopped writing and appeared to be listening with bewilderment. "You're not making sense."

"Okay." I shook my hands in front of me. "Write all this down. After Christine told me Joel had come in to get the strudels, she saw Yaley in the truck, but Yaley didn't come in. Then I took them to the garage where I told Bobby Ray about Yaley after Joel had gone to pump some gas."

"Get on with it." Abby hurried me to the end.

"Fine. Long story short, Joel and Yaley did break up. They did have an argument, according to Bobby Ray, but he doesn't know what about. That said, someone stole Joel's truck. And it had to be fairly early in the morning because Joel took Yaley home between the hours of five thirty and six because that's when Christine had seen them."

"Now we have a little timeline." Abby had drawn a long line on the piece of paper in the notebook and started to denote times and events. "What time did Dottie see Joel—"

"Joel's truck," I corrected her. "About one o'clock."

"According to the news report, Yaley had gone to work. Done some of the tours she was going to add to the schedule. Went to lunch around noon and was supposed to be back for a meeting around one." Abby was writing it all down.

"Also, Yaley was going to meet Joel at the amphitheater for lunch. He didn't show, and it was the last place she was seen. So…" I knew the time of death had to be that hour. "She was killed between noon and one o'clock in the afternoon."

"We need to find out if Joel has an alibi." Abby circled Joel's name.

"In the meantime, I think I need to go visit the Sierra Club." I took the notebook from Abby and stuck it back in my hobo bag. "They need to give me an update on their tours so I can tell my guests." I winked at Abby.

"It sounds like a perfect time to snoop." She grinned. "And I'll keep digging around to see which realtor had filed the complaints against Yaley and her brother."

"I'll see you tonight." I confirmed I'd be at the Laundry Club to go over any more clues we'd collected during the day.

Abby and I took a few more minutes to catch up on books and what was new in our worlds. By the time I left, an hour had passed, and I was starving. It was just about lunchtime down at the Normal Diner, and I knew it was Bourbon Balls and Hot Brown Day. Both of them sounded so good. Thinking about them made my mouth water.

I walked up the sidewalk and waved in the window of the Smelly Dog when Ethel Biddle waved first. She had a fur client on one of the grooming tables with the leash around its neck so the shivering little pup wouldn't try to scamper away.

Not Fifi. She loved going in there to get a spa day. Fifi loved being made over, bathed, groomed, along with having her nails painted. But she also loved romping in the mud, the lake, and the trails.

The Normal Diner was owned by Ty Randal, who was a permanent resident at Happy Trails. Ty and his father actually owned the diner, but his father had taken ill, and Ty had to come back from his big-city chef job to help out around the diner and help his dad raise his brother.

He was one of the good ole southern gentlemen that folks pictured when they stereotyped southern gentlemen.

"Hey there." He waved from behind the pass-through window when he saw me come in and take my seat at the counter stool where I normally sat.

"You on the line?" I asked, even though I could tell by the hairnet on his shaggy blond head of curls. A feature along with his dazzling blue eyes that just amplified his sparkling smile that made the girls swoon.

"I'm making some fresh bourbon balls right now. Ain't that right, Shane?" He nudged the guy next to him.

"New guy? New gal?" I pointed to Shane and the waitress down the counter with the ordering pad in her hand, talking to a customer.

"Shannon is the new waitress." Ty's gaze went blank as if he were going back in time remembering just why he needed a new waitress. Something I desperately have been trying to forget over the past few months. "Pretty good too."

"You don't know Shane?" Sally Ann Dean was sitting right next to me, and I'd not even noticed.

"Sally Ann," I said and lightly touched her arm. "I'm so sorry. I didn't even see you sitting here. My mind has been wrapped up in itself."

"Honey, I can tell. Your nails look like something in the woods got 'hold of them." Her eyes focused on my hand, more specifically my nails. "You better watch it, or that goodlookin' man of yours will get snapped away if you don't start takin' better care of yourself."

"I guess I better call the salon and make an appointment." I referred to Cute-icles, the salon where Sally Ann was a manicurist.

"You better make it fast. Appointments are fillin' up because all the ladies want to make sure their nails look good for Yaley's funeral." Sally Ann sucked in a deep breath. "But Shane, mm-mm." Sally Ann pinched her lips and slowly shook her head. "He's a fine specimen." She leaned over and whispered, "He gets manscaped."

I glanced back up through the window and into the kitchen and saw her observation of Shane wasn't wrong. He had a nice thick head of brown hair that was perfectly cut over his ears and around his neckline. His eyebrows were better groomed than mine. He had tan skin and was a little bit bigger built through the shoulders than Ty.

"Not bad." I wiggled my brows. "Who is he?" I asked her since Ty didn't finish telling me who he was after his thoughts had drifted back in time when he'd mentioned Shannon, the new waitress.

"He owns that new Bourbon Trail Distillery. If you ain't been, it's good." She nodded.

"I heard about it." I watched Shane give Ty a piece of paper. Ty signed off on it, and they shook hands. The two of them said something, and Shane handed Ty a bottle of bourbon.

"Fascinating really." Sally Ann nodded. "I've gotten involved with the Historical Society."

"That's wonderful." I was glad to see Sally Ann taking a vested interest in our area. "My friend Queenie French is the outgoing president."

"I know. I'm thinkin' of runnin' for her spot. So I've been working on making new and interesting things around our area a focal point. Not that it has to do with the history of the Daniel Boone National Forest, but having a distillery come here is a big deal, and bourbon is a rich Kentucky tradition."

"You've got that right." I looked up at Shannon when she finally made it down to me. The girl wasn't quick, but that was okay. I enjoyed talking to Sally Ann.

"What can I get ya?" Shannon asked.

I couldn't help but notice she was a simple woman with short hair laid in what appeared to be a natural wave around her head. She had a plump waist and thick fingers.

"I'm going to have a Kentucky Hot Brown and a side of bourbon balls." The thought of my lunch really made me happy for the first time today.

"Boss, we got bourbon balls ready?" she hollered but didn't bother looking back.

"For Mae, we do." Ty looked at me and winked. "You're going to love the new bourbon."

"Are you Mae?" Shannon asked me with a blank stare, her pen to the pad.

"I am. Welcome to the diner. I love it here." I noticed she was dragging her eyes up and down, giving me the once-over. "I'm a regular."

"Mm-hmm, I've heard about you." She ho-hummed.

"Gosh, I hope it was all good." A nervous laugh escaped me.

"Mostly." She ripped the ticket off the pad and turned around to clip it on the turntable next to the open window where Ty snatched it.

"Mostly." Sally Ann laughed like it was the funniest thing she'd ever heard. "I've got an opening tomorrow if you want to come in." She leaned over again and whispered, "It was Yaley Woodard's appointment, but I'm figuring she ain't coming."

"You knew her?" I asked.

"She was a regular. Paid cash and tipped real good." Sally Ann shrugged. "She liked them blunt-styled nails. Said they were good for back scratching. I'm guessing Joel Grassle ain't gonna get any back scratching anytime soon with him going to the pokey."

"Why would you say that?" I asked.

"Because I saw him pick her up right out there the other day." Sally Ann twisted the stool around and pointed down toward Trails Coffee Shop and Cute-icles. "I was shining up Ann Doherty's nail to a high shine, because she likes them to sparkle when she's counting all that money down at the bank."

"And?" I waved her to continue.

"Joel pulled up. Yaley looked inside and then got in." She took a sip of her water. "I noticed she was a little hesitant before she got in."

"She was?" I gulped and really didn't need her to clarify. "Are you sure it was Joel?"

"Honey, I'd know that truck from anywhere." Sally Ann had said the exact same thing that everyone else said about Joel's truck.

I sat back and let Shannon put my food down in front of me while I considered what Sally Ann had said. Shannon set my bill and Sally Ann's bill next to our plates.

Why would Yaley hesitate? Maybe because Joel said they were meeting at the amphitheater? Why would she need to get in the truck? But Joel said his truck was stolen. Maybe it wasn't Joel driving. Who was it?

I had to find Joel Grassle's truck. But where? It could be hidden anywhere in this forest.

"What time is that appointment?" I asked and raised my fingers toward her.

"Noon. She always came at her lunch break." Sally Ann whipped out some cash and put it down on the ticket for Shannon.

"Nah." I pushed her money back to her. "I'll get it."

"Are you sure? Because your nails ain't gonna be free." She made it very clear.

"I'm positive." I knew a little kindness went a long way, especially when I needed to get some good gossip only a nail and hair salon could give you.

I'm positive Sally Ann got Yaley talking, and I couldn't wait to find out exactly who Yaley Woodard really was.

THE ROAR of sirens blared from the distance. Everyone in the diner turned around to see what all the ruckus was about. When I saw Jerry's sheriff truck zoom past followed closely by Hank's car, I knew it had to be about the case.

"Can I get a to-go box?" I hollered over at Shannon but leaned over the counter and retrieved my own.

Shannon glared at me and started to fuss at me, but Ty told her it was fine.

"It's Mae," Shannon said with sarcasm, making me wonder what I ever did to that woman.

I had no time to worry what her problem was, so I dumped my food in the to-go box and hurried out the door, across the street, through the median, and into the Laundry Club, where I found Betts and Queenie huddled over the police scanner.

"Is it hers?" Queenie looked up at me, her eyes bulging.

"What? Who?" I questioned.

"Shhhh." Betts spat and flailed her hands at us to hush.

"925 off Whiskey Lane. It's a four-door, numbers T-O-U-R-S. Repeat, 925 Whiskey Lane." Agnes Swift's voice was soft-spoken but bold.

"What's a 925?" Queenie asked me, like I would know police code.

I shrugged, tuning out all the other walkie-talkies buzzing in as the deputies gave their locations and who could get there fast enough. My head was churning the numbers Agnes had said.

"Numbers. T-O-U-R-S is not numbers." I chewed on my lip. "Where have I heard—" I gasped. "It's Yaley's car! They found it!"

"Huh?" Queenie jerked back, and Betts followed.

"The license plate number on her flyer is a personal plate that spells tours. She does tours. Makes perfect sense." I opened my bag and pulled out the notebook where I'd folded the flyer and stuck it in there. "See?"

The two of them muddled over the flyer while I hunkered down to see if I could hear anything.

"At the 925," Hank's voice said over the scanner, and the scanner went silent.

"This is big." My eyes shifted between my friends. "I have to go." I took the flyer from them and put it back in the notebook before shoving it back in my bag.

"Where are you going?" Betts asked.

"I've got to go see Joel while Hank isn't at the department." I pushed the door open and trotted down the street to my car at the gas station.

CHAPTER SEVEN

I didn't bother driving the speed limit, but I was cautious as I zipped my car out of downtown and back to the business district. All the deputies were at the 925 from what I'd seen and heard, so I knew it would not only give me time to see Joel, but to talk to Agnes as well.

The parking lot was empty, and when I walked into the entrance of the department, Agnes was sitting on her little stool behind the window, thumbing through today's issue of the Normal Gazette.

When she saw me, she smiled, her saggy jaws tugging up. She was in her eighties, and though she had gray hair and more wrinkles than a shar-pei puppy, she was as spry as anyone I knew. She slid the window open.

"I figured I'd see you down here at some point. Just not figuring on today." Her eyes shifted to the box from the Normal Diner.

"You know I never come empty-handed." My delicious lunch was something I was willing to sacrifice.

She got off her chair and motioned for me to meet her at the door they always kept locked for all the loony people around the national forest, and let me tell you, there were plenty.

"Oh, Hot Brown." She took the box. "We was about to get lunch when the call came in. Are those bourbon balls?"

"They sure are. From bourbon made by Shane Holland, the owner of the new distillery." When I said his name, I noticed she took a sudden interest.

"I think that's who called in the 925." She shuffled back over to her desk and scanned the piece of paper near the walkie-talkie she used to communicate with the deputies. "Yep." Her crooked pointer finger tapped the paper before she gave it a little push over to me.

"I bet when he was going back to the distillery, he saw it," I said to myself and looked at the clock on the department wall.

Shane would've had enough time from when he left the diner to when I heard the sirens and saw the cars zoom out of town to have seen the wrecked vehicle and called it in.

He was, for sure, going on my list of people to talk to. I wanted to know what he saw when he called it in. Probably not much, but I needed to write down everything because I knew Hank wasn't going to tell me anything at this point.

"Say, since Hank is gone, can I see Joel?" I asked her.

"Are you sure you want to go down that path?" she asked. She obviously knew Hank and I had a disagreement. He told her everything. "Hank was pretty upset when he brought Joel to the station, and you'd called that fancy lawyer."

"I know. But Agnes, you know me." I started to plead my case with her. If I could get her on my side, she'd work her granny magic on Hank to at least see my side. Maybe he wouldn't agree, but he'd have a little clarity. "I honestly don't see Joel Grassle killing anyone."

"Mae, dear, his prints are all over the evidence they pulled. Even her purse." Agnes's eyes dipped. "Besides, Jerry wants this case solved as quickly as possible. You know the warmer weather brings out the kids who are busy in the middle of the forest trying to hide their pot fields from the law when we know they're there. Jerry's been desperately trying to stay on top of it, and we are a few men short now that we've got this murder investigation."

"So that means no one is here, and I can see Joel?" I asked.

I knew there were always raids going on in the forest, but generally, the rangers took care of it. Right now and in the fall were when law enforcement was seeking them out.

"I'd like to hear for myself. You know how much he helped me when I first moved here. Not to mention how he'd given Bobby Ray a job for me. I owe it to him to give him the benefit of the doubt."

"Don't breathe a word of this to no one." Agnes's face clouded with uneasiness. I'd never seen that look on her face before, and it made me wonder if she knew something but Hank swore her not to tell me.

I crisscrossed my heart and nodded, following her down the hall and to the holding cell. Joel raised his head. The lines around his eyes were deeper than normal. He ran his hand over his buzz-cut hair and stood up, letting out a long, deep sigh.

"Thanks for calling Ava." He stood up and walked over to the bars.

I looked at Agnes.

"Make it quick." She left no room for discussion. "Joel, you want something to drink?"

"An Ale 8 would be great if you got one." His voice cracked with nerves.

"Sure, honey. I'll be right back." Agnes shuffled back down the hall.

"What is going on, Joel?" I asked him. "It's not looking good." He started to speak, but I shushed him. I took out my notebook. "I'm going to read to you what I know, and then you're going to tell me what you know."

He nodded and leaned up against the bars.

"You and Yaley had gone to The Cookie Crumble that morning. What time did you drop Yaley off and where?" I knew I'd told him I'd let him answer after I told him everything, but now seemed like a good place to fill in those blanks.

"I dropped her off at her house at six o' clock. Her brother was there. He doesn't care too much for me, but I know he'd seen me because he peeled back the curtain." That was some information I could use.

"Had you already broken up by that time?" I asked him.

He closed his eyes, swallowed hard, and sucked in a deep breath.

"Yeah. That's what we were doing all night. We were discussing the breakup. I'm still devastated over it. She broke up with me..." His voice trailed off.

Without even saying it, we both knew this bit of information didn't look or sound good for his case. Angry. Discarded. Hurt. All of those were enough motive to kill someone.

"What did you do next?" I asked him.

"I went over to Steve at the junkyard and picked up the car he needed worked on. I told him I'd just bring it back later that day since I needed to drive it to hear the engine." This wasn't outside of his normal job activities. Many times he'd go pick up a customer's car then bring it back, leaving his truck. "Later that morning, Yaley had called and left me a message on the shop answering machine, asking if we could meet for lunch at the amphitheater. I didn't get the call until it was too late, and Bobby Ray got it when he came in for the day, which was around one o'clock. I left Bobby Ray at the garage and ran down to the amphitheater in hopes she was there, waiting. But she wasn't. I sat down there for an hour or so, just trying to sort through my feelings."

"Did you see or talk to anyone?" I asked him, hoping he'd have someone to give him an alibi.

"No one. I came back to the garage and worked on Steve's car. He called me a few hours after that asking where his car was, and I told him it was up on the lift. He said he'd heard my truck take off about eleven and thought I'd already fixed his car. He said he didn't bother going out to check because he heard the muffler, and it's my normal to just drop and go."

"Eleven?" I wanted to make sure I was writing it correctly on my timeline.

"Yes. I even told Hank that, so I'm guessing he's checking that out." He shrugged.

"Dottie was taking her lunch break, and she said she'd seen you come up in your truck and throw stuff in the dumpster around one." I read off my notes.

"I didn't. It wasn't me." His words were forceful.

"Yaley was in your tarp, and your fingerprints are all over it. Even on her purse," I said, telling him what I knew.

"Of course my fingerprints were on the tarp. It stays in the back of my truck," he gasped, panting in fear. "I handed her purse to her before she got out of the truck that morning. That's how my prints got on it."

"Do you know anyone who didn't like Yaley? Anyone?" I asked.

"No. I told Ava how Yaley was sweet and kind. She and her brother had some issues back when those realtors were going to sue them, but I don't know."

I could feel his anxiety as he talked. It radiated through him and landed on the stress lines of his face.

"I also know that someone saw Yaley get into your truck in front of Cute-icles." My words made his face shoot up.

"You did?" His eyes grew wide. "What about security cameras? Can they see who was driving?"

"I've not gotten that far. I just heard from Sally Ann that she saw Yaley get into your truck around noon. She did say Yaley seemed to hesitate before she got in, but she did. And Hank is off on a call because Shane Holland found her car on the side of the road."

"Shane Holland. I forgot about him." Joel grabbed the bars of the cell. "He and Yaley had an issue. Something about how he was too late getting on the schedule of tours for this season for the Sierra Club. He missed some deadline, and she mentioned something about him getting up in her face and threatening her."

"He did?" This was the first real lead Joel had given me.

"Yeah. And you and I both know that if businesses don't get on these tours, that could be the end of them. Especially a new business." Joel's eyes softened as if there was a glimmer of hope for him yet.

"I brought you some peanuts too." Agnes had walked up undetected because Joel and I were so engrossed in the smallest details of Shane Holland.

"Thanks, Agnes." He took the Ale 8 and the package of peanuts through the bars from her.

"Yes. Thank you, Agnes." I hugged her and smiled at Joel. "You hang in there. I'll keep digging and come back."

"Thanks, Mae!" he hollered after me as I hurried down the hallway. "Bobby Ray was right. You've got a heart of gold."

"We'll see about that," I murmured, bursting out of the door of the department, where a flood of sunlight greeted me.

CHAPTER EIGHT

The last time I'd been to the Daniel Boone National Forest building, where the Sierra Club was located as well as various other park offices, I was involved in finding another dead body. So when I pulled in and parked in front of the old sixties-style brown brick building, shivers covered me from head to toe.

It was also where the office for the National Parks Magazine division was located. Walking into the building, I couldn't help but look at the display of brochures of the various tours, activities, and things to do all lined up.

"May I help you?" the woman asked me from the receptionist desk in the entry.

"Hi. I'm looking for the Sierra Club offices," I said and pointed down the various halls that shot off in all different directions.

"Right down that hallway you'll find their office in the last door on the right." She smiled and picked up the ringing phone. "Daniel Boone National Forest office, how can I direct your call?"

I was happy she didn't point to the hallway where I'd found that dead body in a conference room. That would've just been too much for me.

My phone chirped a swoosh noise from deep within my bag. I knew without looking it was Betts. Since I'd gotten a new phone, I was able to assign different ringtones to suit various people. Betts's just so happened to be the sound of water swishing around in a washing machine.

Hopefully, she was letting me know if she found out anything from her Bible-beater, um, women's group. It could wait, I thought and continued to look for the Sierra Club.

When I opened the door, it was nothing like I'd pictured. There was a big open room with several cubicles. There was a copier along one wall and a long table with what looked like example brochures of different tours they offered. At the end of the table were stacked-up folders each business received at the beginning of tour season with all the details on what tour they were taking.

"Hiya," a woman greeted me. Her eyes, hidden behind a pair of orange-rimmed glasses and curly bangs, popped up over the cubicle. "What can I do for ya?"

"My name is Mae West, and I'm here because I've not heard from my representative about how my brochures are going to be placed for the season." It wasn't a lie. It was just that I'd never met Yaley because it was part of Dottie's job.

We weren't necessarily part of the tours. We were in the Where to Stay program they offered for tourists who called in advance to schedule all their activities before coming to the national park for vacation. They were outside all of the other tourists who found us by our website or the social media campaigns that Abby Fawn did for us.

"Who is your rep? I can look it up in the system." She waved me over but didn't bother getting up.

"Yaley Woodard." I walked up to her cubicle and stepped inside to take a seat in the vacant chair, knowing I was going to be there longer than she anticipated.

Her head jerked up, and she peeled the glasses off her face.

"I'm sorry to inform you, but Yaley is no longer with us." She batted her eyes, looking away as if she were starting to tear up. "As in, she was found dead."

"Oh. Gosh." I eased down into the chair, curling my bag in my lap and cuddling it. "She didn't appear to have an illness."

"Illness? She was murdered," the woman whispered.

"Husband?" I questioned.

"She wasn't married. She had a boyfriend, but he was nice. I think they'd broken up, but I'm not for certain. The morning of the day she disappeared, she was pretty upset about him, but then she got those flowers and called him to meet her for lunch. But she never came back from lunch." She pointed to the cubicle that was kitty-corner to hers.

"That's her office?" I asked and noticed the flowers on the desk.

"Mmm-hmmm," she hummed. "We don't have the heart to even go in there."

"Have the police been here?" I asked.

"They have, but they only talked to my manager. I'm not sure if they went through her desk. It's awful. But in your case, we don't have all her clients moved over yet, but if you give us a few days, someone will be in contact with you. If not"—she put her hand up to her chest—"I'm Diana, and you can call me." She plucked a business card from her desk and handed it to me.

"What did the card with the flowers say?" I asked.

"There was only a simple heart sticker. That's it. Nothing else. That's why Yaley figured it was from her boyfriend because apparently he's not real romantic." Her eyes grew big. "Between me and you"—she leaned closer to me—"I think it was Bert Erickson."

"Who is that?" I asked. "The boyfriend?"

"Bert is a tourist who is in love with Yaley. When he found out that she'd been taken off his normal trail tours, he went crazy. Now this was a few years ago, and now every season, he makes sure he comes in here the first day of the season to get Yaley's tour schedule. He was in here a couple of days before she disappeared, and I saw him hanging around outside on the day she disappeared."

Bert Erickson, Bert Erickson, I continued to say in my head so I wouldn't forget his name. The information Diane was telling me was an incredible lead.

"Did Bert know Yaley had a boyfriend?" I asked.

"I know that he was here when Yaley's boyfriend picked her up one day because Yaley said Bert acted like a baby to her when she told him the tour schedule wasn't out yet. Mentioned something about how Bert made fun of her boyfriend's truck." Diane was definitely talking about Joel.

"Did you ever see Yaley's boyfriend?" I wanted to get into questioning her thoughts on Joel and how he appeared to treat Yaley in front of people.

Not that I thought Joel killed her, but sometimes people were different behind closed doors.

"To be honest, I never met her boyfriend. He would wait outside, but they didn't date for a very long time. Yaley was so excited about him, then something happened, and they broke up." Diane's eyes shifted to Yaley's cubicle and focused on the flowers. "I was going to ask Yaley about it and the flowers at our meeting that day, but she never showed."

"Yaley sounds like a nice lady." I sighed.

"You should know." Diane gave me a cross look. "She worked with you for your tours."

"Yeah. I mean, she sounds nice personally. I didn't know that side of her." I smiled and tried to get back on track. "What was she like to work with? On time? Easy to get along with?"

"She was always on time." Diane stopped. Her eyes narrowed; her bangs fell over them. She put her glasses back on. "Say, you ask a lot of questions. Who did you say you were?"

"I'm Mae West. I own Happy Trails Campground. Yaley comes in to pick up our seasonal brochures, and last time she was in, she talked about how Shane Holland was a big jerk." Okay, so that was a lie, but I was on a mission to find out whatever I could.

"Shane Holland." Diane rolled her eyes, plucked a lollipop out of the cupholder on her desk, then offered me one. I declined. "He thinks he's so great. He thought he could just waltz in here and get on a tour. It don't work that way, and he threw the biggest fit right here."

"He did?" I gasped, more for effect than anything. My phone chirped the sound of a crackling fire, which was Dottie's ringtone.

"Mm-hmm." She raised her chin up in the air before giving a hard nod. "He told her that he'd start his own tour company and put her out of business. He'd have her job, and the Sierra Club would fire her for not taking on his business. It was plum awful."

I dug down into my bag and read the preview of Dottie's text on my phone. It read: *three guests canceled.* I sucked in a deep breath. This meant news about finding Yaley's murdered body in the dumpster at Happy Trails had gotten out, and people didn't want to be camping in the woods when a murderer was lurking around. A little too real-life *Friday the 13th* for most people.

"Really?" The more I heard about this Shane Holland, the more I wanted to make my own tour at the distillery to see exactly where he was the day Yaley disappeared.

"In fact, the meeting that afternoon was about his distillery and the upcoming tours. Bonnie Turner wanted all the brochures to be redone so the distillery was included, but it was only to get back at Yaley because of that whole real estate thing. Bonnie is on our board of directors, and she's the realtor who wanted to sue Yaley and her brother. I think Bonnie should've been kicked off the board because of that. Yaley promised never to do it again, even though she and her brother got in a fight over it. Bonnie refused to step down, and she made Yaley's life a living, well, you know."

Bonnie Turner, Bonnie Turner, Bert Erickson, Bert Erickson, Shane Holland, Shane Holland, I repeated in my head and prayed I wouldn't forget these names.

"Oh, you mean when Yaley and her brother were caught up in the…" I stood up and moseyed over to Yaley's cubicle to get a look at those flowers.

The stamp on the envelope was from Sweet Smell Flower Shop. I knew that place well. And it told me that I'd be able to find out who sent them. Maybe Joel did send them. I'd need to find out.

"Yaley told you about that?" Diane asked and licked on the sucker before she bit off a piece. "She was all hush-hush, but that's when Bonnie demoted Yaley. She couldn't fire Yaley because Yaley was a good worker. And if it was my brother, I'd probably have funneled him all the tourists' business too. I mean, we are loyal to family." She eased back in her chair. "Am I right?"

"You sure are, Diane." I smiled thinking of the gold I'd just struck. I had three names and motives of just why someone other than Joel Grassle would want to kill Yaley Woodard, and I was going to explore them all.

One by one over the next twenty-four hours. Even if I didn't get a wink of sleep, the life of Happy Trails counted on it.

CHAPTER NINE

Bonnie Turner, Bonnie Turner, Bert Erickson, Bert Erickson, Shane Holland, Shane Holland.

"What are you muttering about over there?" Dottie was scrubbing the tub of the bungalow I liked to use for the honeymooners. The big two-person claw-foot tub was in the bedroom, situated underneath the window that faced the sunset over the Daniel Boone National Forest.

It was one of the best views of the full moon in the campground, and in the fall, it was spectacular to sit in a nice long bath with a big glass of champagne as the moon hung over the mountains and the lightning bugs dotted the darkness.

"I'm trying to make sure I recall all the names Yaley's co-worker had told me about. They all had some sort of disagreement or issue with Yaley." I curled the edge of the fitted sheet around the corner of the king-sized bed, ran my hand over the bed until I found the other corner, then tucked it under.

"Issue? If someone killed the woman, they had more than an issue." Dottie groaned and stood up. The long yellow gloves were pulled up past her elbows, and she had a scrub brush in one hand.

With the backside of her other hand, she pushed back the sweaty short hair from her forehead, making it stick up in all directions.

"I don't think we're gonna get this done before we go meet the girls." Dottie pulled the gloves off and took a look at her phone. "We still have the family-of-four bungalow to do."

"What time is it?" I asked her as I threw the sheet up, snapping it in midair to lay perfectly over the bed.

"Near six." She grabbed her cigarette case off the bedside table and took out a smoke. "What is it you got up in that noggin of yours?"

"You go smoke, but call Ty and order all of us a burger platter to go. Call the girls and have them come here instead of the Laundry Club. It's about time for Ty to come home, so have him bring them." It was a good plan. Many times I'd order to go from the Normal Diner when Ty was getting off, so he could just bring it with him.

"The platter with the slaw?" Dottie questioned.

"Yes. Add the slaw." I tried not to smile because I knew she loved Ty Randal's southern slaw. He made it for every BBQ we hosted at the campground, and most of the time, he brought her a little extra to take home. "It ain't no platter without the greasy fries and slaw."

"You got that right." Dottie left the bedroom to head outside.

I moved around the bedroom, fluffing the comforter and positioning the pillows like I'd seen done in *Southern Living Magazine*. It was my go-to magazine when I had decided to make all the bungalows so comfy cozy that people were in awe when they came to stay. It left a lasting impression, and over the last couple of years, the original honeymooners have come back to celebrate their wedding anniversaries with us.

I put fresh candles next to the beds, hung new bathrobes neatly over the side chair next to the tub, and placed the complimentary basket of essential oils, face masks, and other fun items on the floor next to the tub.

The kitchen was a simple eat-in kitchen that I supplied all the utensils for, along with some fun snacks like popcorn, desserts from The Cookie Crumble, coffee from Trails Coffee Shop, and fresh fruits from Mary Elizabeth. She should be dropping off my order sometime this week before the first set of guests arrived.

It reminded me that I needed to talk to Dawn Gentry, Mary Elizabeth's co-owner of the Milkery, about what she might've seen when she was in The Cookie Crumble.

I called Mary Elizabeth and worked around the kitchen to make sure all the things were in place, including the journal I left for guests to write in about their experience, along with any wildlife they encountered or suggestions of places to go for the incoming guests. "Good evening," I said when she picked up. "I'm getting all the bungalows ready, and you know that order I placed?"

"Hi, honey. I'm doing good, thank you for asking." Mary Elizabeth made it well-known that I'd not used the manners I'd learned in etiquette school, which she'd spent a great deal of money on.

"How are you?" I knew better, but I was so anxious to get to the point of my call.

"I said I was doing good. Are you not listening either?" Mary Elizabeth scolded.

"Actually, I'm just so excited to let you know that I have a free morning tomorrow and thought I'd drop by for some breakfast. I mean, you are always asking me to drop by, so I thought I'd come by tomorrow morning, eat, and pick up some of the fruit so you don't have to make a trip out here." So I might've used all this to my advantage, but I still loved her, and with my issue with Hank, I did have some time, though I really wanted to use the extra time to work on my investigation.

"We'd love to have you. In fact, tomorrow is perfect timing." Mary Elizabeth's voice went up an octave with excitement. "It's chicken and waffles at the bed and breakfast tomorrow."

My mouth watered at the mere sound of her freshly made fried chicken and homemade waffles. I swear hers were better than any Cracker Barrel waffles.

"I'll be there around eight if that's okay." It would give me time to get up in the morning and get my head wrapped around going to talk to Dawn and then head to see Shane Holland at the distillery to see what he had to say. Not to mention how convenient it was for him to find Yaley Woodard's car.

Mary Elizabeth and I said our goodbyes right as Dottie walked in to confirm the gals would be here, and Ty would be dropping off the food.

While Dottie went to the office to get some chairs ready for the girls and a pot of coffee brewing, I headed over to the family bungalow with the four bedrooms. Luckily, the only thing I needed to do were the bedrooms, which I took the most time on for the comfort of sleeping.

"Hey, May-bell-ine." Bobby Ray said my name in the most pitiful way from the gravel drive next to the one-bedroom bungalow I let him use for free.

"How did your day go after I saw you?" I could see the stress on his face.

"I couldn't get my head in the game. I nearly slammed my hand in the hood of a car." He shook his head. His long, loose, stringy curls swung down past his ears. I wished he'd get it cut, but he loved his long mullet-style hairdo.

He followed me into the family bungalow.

"That ranger wasn't about to let me in down there."

My head jerked up when he reminded me about the ranger. I'd completely forgotten.

"Oh my gosh!" I took out of the bungalow and ran as fast as I could to the office.

"What in the world has gotten into your crawl?" Dottie popped up with big eyes from a funny position on the floor of the office.

"What are you doing?" I questioned her and noticed there were coffee grounds spilled all over the floor. "Dottie, did you pass out?"

"I'm fine." She held her hand in the air for me to help her up. "Help me."

"Dottie, I don't think you are fine." I pulled her up, placing my arm around her waist to help her to her desk chair. "I think you need to go to the hospital."

"Don't be making no big fuss over me." She batted my hand away once she was sitting down. "I'm light-headed because I'm hungry. It's waaay past my suppertime."

Even after I'd gotten her situated in her chair with a bottled water, her color still wasn't to her. It crossed my mind to call the ambulance, but I'd wait until the gals got here to see what they said. She wasn't going to like me conferring with them, but I didn't care. I loved Dottie.

"Now, what was it that made you run in here as if that big bushy curly hair of yours was on fire?" She might've been pale, but her spunk was still there.

"The ranger. I forgot the ranger was at the front of the entrance. He probably won't let the girls in." My brows knitted.

"It's Newman Weaver." She rolled her eyes. "He's probably already down there snoring. I'm sure they gave him that job because he's old and won't retire. He sits at the National Park office every day and answers the phone. At least, that's what I heard." She raised a shaky finger and pointed to the coffeepot. "I guar-an-tee if you take him a cup of coffee and bat those pretty long lashes of yours that he'll let anyone in here you want."

"Are you sure you're going to be okay?" I couldn't help but notice her hands were slightly shaking. Maybe she was right about not eating, so I grabbed a pack of crackers from the snack closet and took them to her.

"I'll be fine." She waved me off. "I'll just catch my breath, and we can forget all about it."

"Are you sure?" I questioned again because there was no way I was going to leave her alone if she wasn't. The investigation would just have to wait.

"I'm positive. Now git!" she hollered and shooed me away.

With a big cup of coffee in my hands, I slowly walked down the gravel driveway to the entrance of the campground, where Newman was perched in the comforts of his green Kentucky Wildlife truck.

"Hey there, Newman." I held up the cup of coffee. "I thought I'd bring you a cup of coffee while I let you know Betts Hager and the girls are going to stop by and help me get things cleaned up for the guests."

"Mae, dear, I sure would love to let them in, but I've got strict orders from Hank. He especially said you might try to do something to woo me." Newman eyed the coffee and licked his lips.

"Woo you? Aw…" I winked and held the coffee close enough so he'd get a big whiff. "Hank's just worried you might steal me from him," I joked. "But the girls are coming to help me get the bungalows all ready for my guests. With Betts being single now and all, she needs the money to pay her bills, so you know me." I pulled my shoulders to my ears. "I'm doing all I can to help the economy out. I sure would hate for our town to lose the Laundry Club."

If Hank could play this game, so could I.

"I sure hate to hear that about Betts. She's such a nice lady." Newman didn't take his eyes off the coffee. His Adam's apple moved up and down as he swallowed. "I loved hearing her husband preach. Do you think he's delivering in the big house?"

"I'm not sure what he's doing in prison, and I don't think Betts cares either. That's why she's been working her fingers to the bones picking up new cleaning gigs to pay the bills." I waved the coffee a little more so the smell would really get him. "I tried to give her money, but you know Betts. She's too kind and proud to take a handout. If she don't come clean tonight, she won't be able to pay the electric bill."

"How long is it going to take her?" He licked his lips.

"Oh, an hour or two at most." I offered the cup to him.

"Just as long as you limit it to an hour or two." With the coffee in his hands, he took a sip. "I'll see if Darlene has any cleaning needs. We can hire her too."

"She'd love that, Newman. Thank you." I tapped the edge of his car's windowsill before I turned around with a big smile on my face. "Hank Sharp, you can't outwit May-bell-ine Grant West," I muttered under my breath and headed back to the office.

Dottie had gotten the dry-erase board updated with everything I'd discovered about Yaley's relationships between Bonnie Turner, Bert Erickson, and Shane Holland.

"Bert Erickson?" Abby Fawn pulled her leg up in the folding chair after I'd written his name on the whiteboard under the list of suspects. "I know Bert, and I don't think…" Abby stopped and appeared to be gnawing on the possibility.

"According to Diane, Bert has been extremely obsessed with Yaley. If he's as stalkery as Diane claims, he'd definitely know that Yaley had been dating Joel. And if Yaley turned him down all those times, it's a good motive to kill." I shrugged. "All for love."

"I don't know." Abby wasn't convinced. "Keep him on there, but he comes into the library on a fairly regular basis to research various plots of land since he does work for the Property Valuation Department. He loves to hike, and maybe he just likes the tours Yaley had given."

"If he comes into the library, maybe you can ask him a few questions." Betts had the perfect solution that would make Abby happy enough to stay in and not be too upset. "As for Bonnie Turner, I remember her mentioning something a few years ago about the scheme Yaley and Ted had going during a Bible study. In fact, I think she even asked us to put it on the prayer chain."

"You know her?" I questioned.

"I do but not super well. She was not as involved in the group because she worked all the time, showing cabins, properties, houses, you name it. Her phone went off at all hours of the night." Betts's tone was rough with anxiety. "I could see her getting a little upset with Yaley, but still holding a grudge after all these years?"

"What if she has been holding this grudge and waited until the air was cleared before she struck?" Queenie had such a great imagination, and this time it could be true.

"Not bad." I pointed the dry-erase marker at her and turned to write it down as a motive under Bonnie's name.

"The church ladies have been asked to cook the repast food for Yaley's funeral, and I'm sure Bonnie will be there. She never misses a good meal." Betts, though serious, did make us laugh because many people went to repasts just so they could get some good homecooked food at the same time as paying their respects to the family. "Ted had called the church office and asked if the church could host the repast in the undercroft."

"When?" Queenie questioned. "Is it during my Jazzercise class? Because I pay to rent the space, and if I have to cancel class, I won't have happy clients."

"I'm sure the church will call you. I don't know now that I'm just a volunteer and not really head of anything anymore." Betts used to be the heartbeat of the church. She knew all the activities and times, including all the deaths. "We are going to meet late afternoon tomorrow to set up a menu."

"And I can get Mary Elizabeth to make something, so I can come to the meeting. Maybe pick some brains?" I questioned.

"I think it sounds great." Abby looked between me and Betts. "I can see Bonnie holding a grudge against Yaley. Not that it makes her a killer, but just another suspect."

"Perfect." I smiled and quickly wrote our plan underneath Bonnie's name, along with the facts on her motives. "Yaley knocked Bonnie out of a lot of income by funneling all the guests to rent Ted's rental property. Bonnie also planned to sue Yaley, but that didn't go through. Why?"

I wrote "why" in all capital letters and circled it a few times.

"We have Bert Erickson and Bonnie Turner. Who else?" Queenie became a little too jittery if she sat for too long. She got up and shook her hands at her wrists, followed by some gyrating of the legs before she rolled her neck a few times and sat back down.

"Shane Holland, the owner of the new Bourbon Trail Distillery. He and Yaley actually got into an argument because she didn't put him on the tour this season since he didn't file the paperwork in time."

"That's his fault," Abby pointed out. "Right, Queenie?"

"Mmm-hhmmm." Queenie nodded. "When I was in the filing department for the park, they were strict. No exceptions, even if the tour was going to bring in a lot of money. They get all sorts of state grant money, and it's been distributed way before the season starts.

Shane Holland should've researched that before he opened and had the proper paperwork in place."

"It might be his fault, but he might not see it that way." There was one thing I could count on when looking at possible murder suspects, and that was how nothing was ever as it seemed. "In fact, he was the one who found Yaley's car wrecked on the side of the road."

I quickly made bullet points on the board and jotted down exactly why Shane would have motive.

"Dottie?" I questioned Dottie's silence. "That's it." I slammed the marker on the desk when I noticed she was looking as gray as a corpse. "We are going to the emergency room."

"No," Dottie insisted. "I'm fine."

"You are not fine." I turned to the gals because I knew we'd be stronger in numbers, and if they knew what had been going on with Dottie, they'd make her get checked out. "Dottie has passed out or almost passed out a couple of times these past two days, and we need to get her to the emergency room."

"I was wondering what was going on with your color." Queenie got out of her folding chair and took a hard look at Dottie's face. "It's them cigarettes. I told you."

I gathered up my bag and Dottie's purse.

"Don't be going and giving her the business." Betts walked over and helped Dottie up, scolding Queenie. "The last thing she needs is a fussing from any of us. Come on, Dottie. We will get you looked at and back in no time."

"Don't y'all be making a fuss over me. I'm fine." Dottie shifted her glare to me.

You know the saying, *if looks could kill*...well.

CHAPTER TEN

Dottie's initial vitals had checked out okay. They weren't the best, and her blood sugar levels were off the chart low. The emergency room doctor had ordered Dottie to stay overnight for observation or maybe even longer, depending on what the full blood workup panel showed.

There was a lot of tossing and turning all night with thoughts of how she was doing. Plus, when I'd heard someone driving past my camper in the middle of the night, I looked out the window and saw it was Hank.

Like a creeper, I watched him go into the camper he rented from me and come back out with Chester.

"Come on, Fifi." I threw the covers off me, pulled on a sweatshirt over my nightshirt, and put on a pair of sweatpants, along with my hiking boots by the door. "Let's go see Chester."

Hank was walking Chester past my camper when we finally made it outside. It took me a minute to try and tame my hair so I would look somewhat presentable for Hank.

"What are you doing up?" Hank asked, stopping at my door when he saw me open it.

"Can't sleep." I watched Fifi run down the steps and straight over to

Chester. They did the usual sniffing around each other before they followed behind me and Hank. "Dottie had some fainting issues, but I think it's her blood sugar. The girls and I took her to the emergency room. They kept her overnight for observation."

"I'm sorry, Mae." Hank's words were soft and sincere. "Can I do anything?"

"No. I think I've got her covered." I walked beside him with my hands clasped in front of me, feeling a little awkward since we normally held hands or fussed over the dogs not being on leashes, but I could sense our relationship was on his mind as much as it was on my mind. "Are you going to be mad at me forever?"

"I think I'm never going to be okay with you wanting to snoop around every chance I have an investigation," he said matter-of-factly.

"It's only when it affects people I love." I couldn't compromise my beliefs. "I know you felt as though I took Joel's side over you when I asked Ava to come help him, but it's not the case at all." I put my hand out for him to stop walking. He turned to me.

When he looked down at me, my heart felt an ache that I'd never felt before. A breaking into pieces in that one instant. I could see the pain in his eyes.

"You and I both want the killer brought to justice. You love Normal just as much, if not more, than I do. I want to help Joel. I want to help everyone. I want my business to thrive so our community can thrive. I want us to thrive, Hank. Why can't we just work together?" I asked him. "You were so good about it when we went back to Perrysburg."

Not that I wanted to be reminded of why we'd gone back to my hometown a few months ago, but I had to put on my sleuthing cap there, and he was accepting of it.

"I needed you to introduce me to people. I didn't know people there, and we were there to get to the bottom of things." He didn't take his hard stare off of me.

I looked away. Fifi and Chester were right there with us. They must've known we were in a serious discussion because they weren't running off to smell the midnight scents and various critters that could be out.

"You trusted me then, why not now?" It seemed like a legitimate question. "I have good resources to help you. In fact, Yaley and Shane Holland had gotten into a fight, and he just so happened to find her car?"

"How did you know that?" Hank's brows V'd.

I gulped.

"Granny," he murmured. "I knew there was a reason I'd not heard from you, or maybe you stopped in to talk to Joel."

I curled my lips from saying anything, but even with the dark of the night and bright moonlight, Hank could see right through me.

"Geez, Mae." He threw his hands up in the air. "You've talked to him."

"And you and I both know it's very possible his truck was stolen. Did you go to the junkyard and ask Steve about it?"

"Of course I did, Mae." Hank put his hands on his hips and moved his tongue around in his mouth as his jaw set firm. "You're not going to back off, are you?"

"It's not that."

He shifted, so I came clean. "No. I simply don't think Joel did it, and I can't even begin to let the campground go bankrupt while the Normal Sheriff's Department twiddles their thumbs by looking at one person." I gave a loud whistle. "Let's go, Fifi."

I wasn't sure if it was sheer exhaustion that had me at my wits' end or the worry about Dottie and Hank, but I wasn't going to just sit idly by like a good girlfriend.

Without another word, I started my stomp back to my camper with the pitter-patter of not only Fifi but Chester following me closely behind.

"Chester!" Hank's voice echoed through the darkness. "Chester, stop!"

"Come on, Chester." I gave a little click of the tongue to make him keep following me. "Want a treat?" I asked, knowing I was going to make Hank deal with me one way or another.

"Mae, you can't hold my dog hostage." Hank's voice got louder and so did his footsteps.

"I'm not holding anyone hostage." I turned on a dime, and Hank practically ran into me. "I'm simply walking back to my home to go back to bed."

"This is what I love best and hate most about you." He shook his head. "I love how you stand for what you believe in but hate when I'm at the other end. It's a very difficult position for me to be in."

"I recall how we sat right over there a year or so ago." I pointed over his shoulder to the bank along the lake. "And we both agreed this would get complicated. Here we are. Hank Sharp," I said his name with a stern voice, "this is the time it's going to get complicated. Either we are worth fighting for, or we aren't. You pick because I'm still right here."

I marched up the steps with a hopeful twitch in my gut that he'd stop me and pull me toward him, telling me I was worth every single ounce. But once I made it up the steps, I hesitated slightly on turning the knob of the camper door.

Nothing.

Fifi and Chester ran into the camper as if it was family as usual, and I shut the door behind me.

"Mae, open up." Hank's voice came from the other side of the door, making me smile.

I forced the grin from my face and flung open the door. Hank was leaned up against the doorframe.

"Fine. Let's make a plan that'll keep us both happy because I can't stop you from snooping, and I can't stop my heart from loving you." He took a step inside of the camper and drew me to him. "I swear, one of these days, I'm going to regret giving in to you."

"No, you won't. You'll always protect me. Even from the likes of Shane Holland." I looked up and kissed him.

Chester and Fifi were pretty happy. Both of them danced around our feet and hopped up on the couch after Hank sat down. I retrieved my hobo bag and dug out the notebook. I'd let Hank know the things I already knew.

"Okay." He looked up, crossed his ankle over his other leg, and held on to it. "Tell me what you've got."

"Right now?" I looked at the time. "It's two in the morning."

"And what do we have to do?" he questioned.

He might've been willing to work with me due to the fact he loved me, but I could see right now that he wasn't going to make it easy on me.

"Besides, when there's an investigation going on, time doesn't exist. You do understand that even though it might appear we aren't doing anything, we really are." A sly smile crossed his lips.

"Great!" I said enthusiastically and opened the notebook instead of just handing it to him. "Joel had dropped his truck off at Steve's in exchange for Steve's car since he was going to work on it."

Hank rolled his hand around as if he wanted me to skip that part.

"Okay, Yaley and Joel had been up all night, contemplating their relationship before they broke up. Then they got donuts, and he took her home." The scenario began to play in my head, and Hank completely disappeared as I paced back and forth. "She went home to get ready for work, went to work, got the flowers, and called Joel to meet him because she thought he'd sent her flowers when he really didn't. Whoever sent her flowers stole Joel's truck because they knew she would meet up with Joel, and it worked." I smacked my hands together. "She knew the person who stole the truck because Sally Ann said she hesitated before she got into the truck."

"Sally Ann?" Hank all of a sudden got interested. "Sally Ann saw Yaley get abducted?"

"Yes. No. Yes." I waved my hand back and forth. "Sorta. I mean, Sally Ann told me she was doing Ann's nails, and they saw Joel's truck, but not if it was Joel in the truck." I made sure he knew that little bit of information. "Yaley walked up to the truck but hesitated when she looked in. Something or someone said something to her to get her into the truck. That someone had to be the person who sent her flowers."

"How do you know about the flowers?" Hank obviously hadn't talked to Diane.

"I went to the Sierra Club because they've not picked up my brochures to hand out." I didn't technically lie, but he knew what I was getting at. "I asked Diane, the girl who works with Yaley in the office, about Yaley. She mentioned how Yaley said she and Joel had broken up, but Yaley was on the fence and very happy after the flowers were sent. I looked at the flowers, and there wasn't a name on them. She thought they were from Joel. They weren't."

"Sally Ann couldn't ID the driver?" Hank asked.

"She didn't look hard enough because she assumed it was Joel driving Joel's truck. But it wasn't."

"Whoever killed Yaley knew Joel sometimes used Happy Trail's dumpster and knew that his muffler was loud enough to get attention that told us it was him without making us look too close. Same with Dottie. She heard the muffler, glanced outside, and saw it was him, not thinking another word about it." My words made Hank's brow rise.

"So I'm not sure it was Shane Holland. After all, he's pretty new to the community, and I've never seen him in the campground. Though he and Yaley had the most recent fight." I gnawed on my cheek. My eyes darted back and forth. "Who could've seen the fight? Diane said it was in the office, and guess who works in the office."

"Who?" Hank played along.

"Bonnie Turner." I flipped to the page in the notebook where I'd written down all the motives Bonnie would have to kill Yaley and handed it to Hank. While he scanned the page, I told him, "She was the realtor who had filed the lawsuit against Yaley and her brother. Do you remember that?"

"I was a full-time ranger when it happened, but we've opened the documents. They came to an agreement, but I'm not sure how that went down, so we are going to question Bonnie." Hank was actually giving me some information.

"She might give me more, or Betts." I shrugged.

"Tell me what you've already got planned." Hank patted the seat next to him, even though Fifi was curled up there. He picked her up and put her in his lap.

I ended up sitting next to him, telling him all the plans the Laundry Club ladies and I had come up with. The next thing I knew I was blinking awake and the morning sun was shining right in the camper windows.

CHAPTER ELEVEN

"I can't believe I just fell asleep." I sipped on the cup of coffee Hank had handed me.

"One minute, you were talking with your head on my shoulder, then the next thing I knew, you were silent." He smiled from behind the cup before he took a sip. "I looked down at you, and you were out. So I grabbed a few covers, thinking you'd wake up, but you never did. Not even when I left apparently."

"I can't believe you came back this morning. And fixed me coffee." I sucked in a deep breath of gratitude. "Thank you. I think the stress of Dottie got to me."

"You can take Joel off your stress list. Ava Cox found a witness during the time Yaley disappeared. She was walking her dog in the median and actually talked to Joel, and he forgot about it. But the woman came forward and said she'd talked to him. So it's an alibi, not completely solid. And…" He leaned against the counter and appeared to be freshly clothed and well rested. "I'm giving you back the campground."

"Really?" I squealed and jumped to my feet so I could put my coffee down to hug him.

"Really. I think we've gotten all the evidence we could collect. I've already put out an APB on the truck, and it's extended to multiple states. We have got surrounding forces looking into video cameras and junkyards to see if it was junked." He pushed off the counter and refilled his Yeti coffee cup. "I've got to get going. What is your plan today? So I know where you are at all times."

"I'm going to go work in the office since Dottie isn't here." I reached over and grabbed my phone, checking to see if anyone had called me from the hospital to come get her. "Then I'm going to take Fifi on another walk before I head out to make my rounds at the Bourbon Trail Distillery and Cute-icles to get my nails done. After that, I'm heading over to the church undercroft to help with Yaley's repast while listening in for some good gossip that just might lead to a clue."

"You know that we don't take time off to get nails done." Hank thought he had me.

"No, but two people at Cute-icles saw Yaley get into Joel's truck right before she was killed, so I'm going to smile and get my nails done while I partake in a little gossip." I winked. "Hank Sharp, don't you know that we southern women love to gossip about other people's issues, and honey, I think Yaley Woodard had more issues than *Southern Living* has ever printed."

"Oh, Mae, don't make me regret this." He kissed the top of my head and gave the dogs a nice scratch on their heads before he bolted out the door for the day.

I filled the dog bowl with food and let the fur kids eat while I grabbed a much-needed shower and got ready for the day. There wasn't much I could do for my hair other than let it dry by itself. If I wanted to dry it, then I'd have to either get a professional blowout to help tame the frizz from me trying to blow dry it or spend the next hour trying to flat iron the heck out of it. Neither of those would get me closer to what I needed to do today, and that was to get some answers to the clues the Laundry Club ladies and I had found.

"Are you two ready to get the messages off the machine, then go for a walk?" Just the tone of my voice made Chester and Fifi dance with excitement.

The sun had already popped up over the mountains and nestled itself in what appeared to be a crystal-blue-sky day. It was a great day to run around the park and visit with people I needed to see.

The campground was quiet. Bobby Ray's car and Ty's car weren't in their driveways. Henry was in the motorized pond boat with the moss rake. His whistling echoed off the surrounding trees, which made me smile and made the dogs run to the edge of the pond. Luckily, they didn't jump into the water. I had no time to give them baths this morning.

Henry waved from the little green boat. He loved going around to make sure the wildlife as well as his little forest of cattails were healthy. He would also check the fountain in the middle to make sure it was at peak performance since it was the only irrigation for the body of water.

Walking past Dottie's house reminded me to check my phone again just in case I'd missed a call from the hospital. Nothing.

Fifi and Chester darted ahead of me and went straight to the office door.

"Gosh." I laughed. "Am I that predictable?" I stopped when I noticed the office door was cracked.

Chester pawed at the door to let himself in.

"Chester," I called to him in a whisper and bent down so he'd run over for a scratch. "Good boy." Fifi and Chester both ran over to me. I grabbed them both by the collar and tugged them both up into my arms.

The sound of the filing cabinet drawers opening then shutting made my heart beat so fast. I slid my body along the outside wall of the office and turned the corner to look into the window to see who was in there. Only Dottie, Henry, and I had a key. Dottie was in the hospital. Henry was at the lake, and I obviously wasn't in there.

The blinds were closed from when we'd locked up yesterday, so I couldn't see inside. A loud whistle made me look over at Henry. He was giving me a strange look. I gave him the silent come-here nod. I tried to nod toward the building to tell him someone was in there without talking.

When he shifted the lever on the boat to move it to the bank of the lake closest to me, I realized he knew what I was trying to tell him.

Luckily, Fifi was a tiny little thing, so she wasn't breaking my arm, but Chester...shoo wee. He was definitely the size of a small child. I adjusted him a few times before Henry made it over to me.

"Someone is in there," I whispered into Henry's ear. His wiry head tickled my nose. "Dottie is still in the hospital."

I watched as Henry studied my face, not speaking a word. He pulled up his pant leg and exposed his ankle gun, which he kept on him at all times. Slowly, he bent down and unsnapped it. He stood up with one hand on the gun and one finger to his mouth, telling me to be quiet. I nodded in agreement.

He held his hand out for me to stay put and slowly turned to go back to the front of the office. There was a momentary panic that riddled my insides. Fifi must've felt it. She twisted her head to my face and began to lick me. I moved my head back and forth, which made Chester squirm. His back claws stabbed me in my side, making me drop him.

He scurried around the building.

"Chester," I gasped and held Fifi tight to me. I bolted around the side of the door just as Henry was kicking it in, and Chester ran inside. "No!"

"What the—" I heard someone screaming from inside. "Henry Bryan! You've lost your ever-loving mind! I oughta take that gun and pistol-whip you back to the hole you crawled out of!"

"Dottie?" I hurried inside the office only to find Dottie had the gun on Henry. "How did that happen?"

"She grabbed my gun," Henry cried out with his arms trying to cover his head.

"Dottie, what are you doing here?" I put Fifi down and pushed the gun out of Henry's way. "You're supposed to be at the hospital."

"They let me out last night, and I got me a cab home." She gave Henry one last long glare before she handed his gun over to him. "I swear, you point that thing at me again, and it'll be the last thing you ever point at anyone." She pointed to the door. "You git on outta here before I knock you into next week."

"Calm down, Dottie. I told him someone was in here, and you were at the hospital, so I thought someone had broken in. I'm sorry, Henry. Thank you." I patted him on the back when he walked past me. "How were we to know you were home? So?"

"So what?" She went back to looking in the filing cabinet. "I'm pulling all the guest folders who have left messages about canceling their reservation due to the murdered body found on the campground."

"Are you kidding me?" I let out a big sigh that held relief there wasn't a robber and stress about the cancellations.

"Does it look like I'm kidding?" Dottie swirled her finger around her face.

She was in one of those moods. The mood told me she wasn't in any shape to do anything but get work done.

"Why are you here? Why don't you go home and rest today?" I suggested before she gave me a look that told me to be quiet and that she was going to do what she wanted to do. "Fine. Work. But I have to know what the doctor said and why they let you go."

"They said everything looked good. Keep an eye on my sugar intake. That's it." She shrugged and put the stack of files on her desk before she sat down and started to type on the keyboard. "I'll get these guests' down payments refunded because I'm guessing you're not going to argue with why they are canceling."

"I really hate this." I eased down into the chair. Chester and Fifi sat patiently next to Dottie's chair in anticipation of her throwing them a treat.

"I know, but that's another reason why I came in. If I'm in here doing this piddly work, you can go out there and carry on with the plan the Laundry Club gals put together." She opened the treat jar and took a couple out, handing them to the dogs.

"And you feel up to it?" I wanted to make sure before I did anything.

"I'm fine." She looked at me with big eyes and a set jaw. "Now go leave me be, and I'll take care of the dogs."

"Only if you're sure, because this campground means nothing to me compared to you and your health." It was true. "I've been bankrupt once, and I don't mind doing it again."

"Go!" She gave a hard point to the door.

"Okay." I looked at the dogs, who were more than happy to be here with Dottie. "I'll come back before I go to the undercroft and take them for a walk."

"Mmm-hhhmm." Dottie was focused on the computer screen and didn't even look up to tell me goodbye.

CHAPTER TWELVE

"In the middle of the night?" Mary Elizabeth fingered the strand of pearls around her neck. Her shoulder-length straight hair screamed at me. I ran my hand down my curls and let the ping of jealousy settle in my gut. Poor Mary Elizabeth had done all she could for my hair when I was an awkward teenager. "I've never heard of any hospital releasing anyone in the middle of the night."

She confirmed everything I thought about Dottie being discharged from the hospital.

"I guess if you've got someone like Dottie Swaggert snapping at you, then you might let her get out of there as quick as possible." Dawn Gentry set the plate of chicken and waffles down on the table before she sat down to join me and Mary Elizabeth.

"I bet she was a pill. But I'm telling you," I cut a piece of chicken and stabbed it along with a piece of waffle before I dipped it into the maple syrup, "she's got something going on other than a low blood sugar level. She's been pale for the better part of the past couple of days even after she eats. She's unsteady on her feet and stubborn as all get out."

"Honey, she's a grown woman." Mary Elizabeth's southern accent poured out of her. "All you can do is continue to check on her. After that, it's up to her to take care of herself. And those cigarettes don't help her at all."

"Has she ever tried to stop smoking?" Dawn asked. She had her head rested in the palm of her hand, her arm propped up on the table. Her fingernails picked at the edge of her pixie cut. She'd kept her black hair short since I'd known her over the past couple of years and stayed true to her skinny jeans, black t-shirts, and her black leather jacket.

"Not that I know of." I shrugged and took in the difference between Dawn and Mary Elizabeth while we sat there in silence and stuffed our faces.

The two business partners couldn't be more polar opposites. Mary Elizabeth was always decked out in Lilly Pulitzer outfits and her strand of pearls, making her the picture-perfect image of a southern woman. And she loved playing that part, though it wasn't a part. She was southern through and through.

"This is the best yet." I put the last bite in my mouth and closed my eyes to savor it.

"You say that about every meal I make." Mary Elizabeth's voice held pride.

"How's the Milkery doing?" I asked as I geared up for the real reason I was here, which was to question Dawn about seeing Joel and Yaley.

Even though Hank told me Joel had been released with a flimsy alibi and eyewitness, I'd already planned to stop by here, and I wasn't going to cancel on chicken and waffles ever. Besides, Dawn might've had some other insight or views that might come in handy.

"Great. We got some new calves and some milking mamas. Plus the goat milk and soap sales have tripled since this new goat-milk-and-cheese fad some of these health nuts have tapped into." Dawn picked at the edges of her fingernails.

"It's not a fad," Mary Elizabeth corrected. "Some people are lactose intolerant, and we are here to provide them what they want."

"Speaking of diets and stuff, I heard you were at The Cookie Crumble picking up donuts the morning Yaley Woodard disappeared and found her way into my dumpster." I tried to make light of the situation, but there was no denying it was still very real.

"Yeah. Creepy." Dawn's body did a shimmy-shake. "I didn't know her, but I saw her in Joel's truck, and from what I heard, he's a suspect."

"He's not." I sat there for the next twenty minutes, telling Mary Elizabeth and Dawn everything I'd found out and that'd happened over the past twenty-four hours, including the little hiccup with Hank and how I was going to look into Shane Holland, Bonnie Turner, and Bert Erickson. "Do you remember anything odd about the situation or see anyone out of place there that morning?"

"Is Bert Erickson that guy who does all the trail runs?" She looked at Mary Elizabeth.

"He is. He's a doll." Mary Elizabeth thought everyone was a doll, including killers. "He runs the trail behind the Milkery. In fact, he was on the trail the day the girl disappeared."

"Which trail?" I questioned.

"You know. The one that goes down to the river then up to your place. It's like three miles or something. Who on earth would want to run something like that? It's all bumpy." She used her hand to make bumps in the air. "It was the first time I'd seen him on that trail this season."

"You said that morning?" I questioned, trying to get a timeline.

Dawn Gentry appeared to have gone into deep thought.

"What is that look?" Mary Elizabeth shook a finger at me. "I know that look. You think he might've killed that poor girl."

"Like I told you, he only took Yaley's tours, and something upset him this time. I'm not sure what, but if you take all of someone's tours, that tells me you're a little obsessed with that person." I picked up my plate and stood up so I could put it in the dishwasher. "I just need to find him so I can question him about his whereabouts."

"I told you his whereabouts. He was running the trail that morning." Mary Elizabeth took my plate from me and added it to the pile she already had on the counter from the breakfast for the guests who were staying at the Milkery Bed and Breakfast.

Not everyone who liked to visit the Daniel Boone National Forest liked to stay in a camper, tent, or outside, period. When Mary Elizabeth and Dawn had the idea to convert the old farmhouse on the Milkery Dairy Farm to a bed and breakfast, it was their best business decision yet.

With Mary Elizabeth's money and Dawn's business sense, it made their unlikely union a perfect partnership.

"He was acting strange." Mary Elizabeth nodded. "I was out checking on the radishes because they are planted out by the trail, and when he passed, I waved to him. He gave a slight twitch of the hand. Normally, he stops and chats a bit, but not that morning. But the next day, he was as chatty as ever."

"I saw him." Dawn smacked the table. "I saw him at The Cookie Crumble that morning."

"What?" I twisted my body around, my jaw dropping. "You did?"

"Yes. Now that I think about it. I saw him leaning up against the parking lot light. I thought I recognized him, but it was still dark out, and the light cast a weird shadow on him." She drew her eyes up to meet mine. "Do you think he killed her?"

"If he thought she was with Joel, maybe he followed them, and then followed Joel. He stole Joel's truck, sent her flowers as Joel, and that's when he abducted her. He ran the trail before he picked her up not only so you would see him, but to make sure he scoped out the campground because somehow he knew Joel used it." I could see the puzzle pieces falling together, though some parts were really sketchy. It was a start. "Do you mind if I get out of here? I think I need to call Hank. He might come talk to you."

"Yeah." Dawn nodded. "That's fine. I'll tell him everything I saw."

With quick goodbyes and hugs all around, I decided that I would call Hank and tell him what Dawn and Mary Elizabeth had told me while I took my own little walk on the trail Mary Elizabeth had seen Bert running on the morning Yaley disappeared.

"I told her you'd probably call her or something." I kept my eyes peeled on the ground for any sort of evidence from Bert, but it was the usual trash some hikers left behind.

"She's sure it was Bert Erickson?" Hank asked for verification.

"Yes." I didn't tell him my full theory because he had his way of thinking, which was the real-cop-school way. Mine was the common sense kind of sleuthing, so I'd let him come up with his own time frame for how Bert had pulled it off. "Now you have him pretty much placed at the scene of the body. Not necessarily at the campground but within a couple miles of the dumpster."

"Good work, Mae." Hank approved. "This is the kind of sleuthing I like you doing. Getting some gossip or bits of truth and passing it along to me."

I watched my step as the sunlight filtered through the trees' leaves, creating shadows and dotting the path.

"Now go try to find Bert yourself. That's something the old sleuthing Mae would do." Hank continued to praise me.

"Hold on! Bumpy ahead! Don't fall out! Whooooohoooo!" A voice screamed through the thick wooded area with the sounds of rushing water muting most of the screams.

"Mae? What is that yelling?" Hank paused. "Are you on the trail?"

"I had to see for myself. I've not been on this one side of the trail, and Mary Elizabeth is right." I looked through the trees and saw Skip Toliver taking a whitewater rafting group down one of the rapids. "That noise is a scared tour group with Skip. And if you cross the river, you'll find the Red Fox Trail that leads straight up to Happy Trails Campground."

I followed my directions with my eyes across the river and over to the beginning of where I knew the trail was located. I looked away when something caught the sun's rays perfectly and shined right into my eyes.

"Mae? You there?" Hank asked when I abruptly stopped talking.

Carefully, I climbed over a large oak tree that had fallen and covered part of the trail to see what the shiny object was. With my eyes on it, I bent down and pushed away some of the brush covering it. My eyes grew big. My mouth opened. My mouth closed.

"H-H..." I tried to say Hank's name. "I-I..."

"Mae, what is it?" Hank asked.

"I found a gold chain." My eyes focused on the special heart links. "And it looks exactly like the one missing from Yaley's body."

The next day he was as chatty as ever, Mary Elizabeth's words rang in my ears.

"Send me a pin of your location." Hank was talking about the ability to use the GPS location on my phone to send him the exact location of where I was so he could get to me...or rather, the gold chain.

I sat down on the trail with my knees pulled up to my chest. I rocked back and forth, staring at the chain.

"It has to be her chain." It wasn't unusual for me to talk to myself during times of high stress or even when I was trying to figure out an investigation.

Hearing myself helped me sort out various theories, and seeing this specific chain wasn't a theory. I was positive about it. In my head, I'd already pictured Bert at The Cookie Crumble. I could visually see him leaning up against the light pole with his arms crossed, glaring at Joel's truck. I didn't even know what Bert looked like, but in my head, I did. Or at least a shadow of him. Then my mind played the image of a man running the trail and sweet Mary Elizabeth waving to him with her hands in her gardening gloves. I could even see the look on her face when he didn't wave back.

I could almost hear his feet pounding on the earth as he jogged down the trail, not even stopping, and without a care in the world, casually tossing the chain into the woods as though no one would ever find it. Little did he realize there are always eyes watching in the woods. I was watching.

I jumped when I heard feet running. My heart stopped, thinking it was him. He'd heard someone found the necklace and was going to find me. Stop me from turning it over.

"Hank." I leapt to my feet and practically threw myself into his arms.

TENTS, TRAILS, & TURMOIL

"Are you okay?" He hugged me tight. "I've not seen you this shaken up before, even after you've found a body."

"I just can't wrap my head around this man being so close to Mary Elizabeth. The thought that he knows my family. Knew my campground." I let go and felt a comfort when I looked into his eyes. "I'm so lucky to have you."

I wrapped my arms back around him and let him comfort me by rubbing down my hair and back.

"The necklace is right there." I pointed over beyond the fallen tree, the sunlight still lighting up the dainty chain.

Hank dug into his pants pocket, and with the fling of his hand, he brought the evidence bag to full length. He took a pair of blue latex gloves from his back pocket and slipped them on his hands. He climbed over the dead tree and stood over the necklace.

I watched him work as he squatted down, using his flashlight to light up various spots around the chain as if he was looking for prints or anything else that might be part of the evidence. He took his cell phone out and snapped a few photos before he finally picked up the simple heart-link chain to place in the plastic evidence bag.

After he sealed it, he held it up near his face and took a good look at it.

"I think you're right. This looks like the chain, but no heart pendant." He looked over his shoulder at me. "I think we need to shut down the trails. I'll call the park rangers to let them know what we found."

"I can't even imagine what this is going to do to our tourism." My insides gnawed at the anger I was feeling toward Bert Erickson. "Do you even know where to find this guy?" I asked Hank and watched him climb back over the tree.

"We've got some people on it." Hank's eyes softened, and he smiled, slightly shifting his head to the side. "Are you sure you want to continue to look into things?" His eyes were filled with concern. "You've already done enough. I mean, this necklace is a fantastic piece of evidence." Hank held the bag in the air.

The simple chain had found its way into the corner of the plastic bag, like a snake curled up for safety.

"I'm fine." I was much better knowing Hank felt confident they would be able to find him. "I know you're going to bring him to justice."

"Mae, I'm not for sure Bert Erickson is the killer. We still have to bring him in for questioning, and he might have an alibi." Hank was supposed to make me feel better, not worse.

"Then it looks like I still need to go to the Bourbon Trail Distillery and get my nails done to see if anyone noticed anything else while you go find Bert." I leaned over and kissed him on the cheek before the other set of footsteps I heard coming down the trail reached us.

Before I knew it, we were swarmed with deputies from the Normal Sheriff's Department and a couple of the park rangers. A few of them already had the metal detectors turned on, looking for what I assumed would be the heart pendant.

I headed back to the Milkery, only to find Mary Elizabeth at the mouth of the trail, talking to a ranger. Her hand was over her mouth as though she were in shock.

"Are you okay?" she asked me when I came into sight. "I heard you found something. What?"

"I think I found Yaley's necklace," I told her and curled my arm in the crook of her elbow, leading her back to the bed and breakfast. "I can't help but wonder if Bert Erickson stalked Joel and Yaley that morning. He stole Joel's truck, and when Yaley was hesitant to get into the truck, he said something to Yaley to get her to go with him. And she got in because she knew Bert. He killed her and disposed of her body in the dumpster. But why would he take her necklace?"

"Maybe she struggled, and it came off." Mary Elizabeth had a good point. "There he is! Help! Killer!" Mary Elizabeth squealed and pointed to another trail leading deep into the park where a tall, dark-haired man in running shorts and no shirt was jogging.

The ranger bolted toward the man, who looked around and took off. The ranger had his mouth up to his walkie-talkie and was following after Bert. Mary Elizabeth and I stood there, watching a few of the deputies emerge from one trail and bolt down the other.

"Now what?" Mary Elizabeth asked Hank. She wrung her hands together.

"We hope they get him, and we cuff him to take him in for questioning." Hank kept his eyes on the trail in anticipation that they'd emerge from the woods any minute now.

"Questioning?" Mary Elizabeth didn't like Hank's answer. "He is running from the law. Isn't that a sign of guilt?"

"We can't assume anything, Mary Elizabeth. We have to make sure we have enough evidence and also play by the rules. Everything has to be by the book, or he could get a great lawyer that could find one little thing to get him off." Hank's chin rose in the air, and he postured a little taller when two deputies dragged Bert Erickson out of the woods.

Each of them had him by the arm. Bert flailed his shoulders, not cooperating.

"What on earth is wrong with you people?" he spat as he got closer to Hank.

"Why don't you two go on?" Hank instructed me and Mary Elizabeth. "Take him on down to the department. I'll be there directly," Hank told the deputies. They dragged Bert off toward the Milkery parking lot. "I'll call you," Hank told me and gave my arm a squeeze.

He was in full-on detective mode, and I knew he needed to go do his work.

"Call me when you hear something." Mary Elizabeth gave me a quick hug before she headed back into the kitchen door of the old farmhouse.

When I got back into the car, I called to check on Dottie. She said she was feeling fine. I wasn't even going to tell her about Bert and the necklace, but it was too late. She'd already gotten a call from Betts. She and Abby had heard it over the scanner while having their morning coffee at the Laundry Club.

Since both of them knew, I called them on my drive over to the Bourbon Trail Distillery.

TONYA KAPPES

"Why are you going there now?" Betts had me on speakerphone, and I could hear myself echo.

"Yeah. If Hank feels like they have the killer in custody, I agree with Betts," Abby said, putting in her two cents.

"Hank said they had to question him. Just because Dawn saw Bert the morning of Yaley's death and thought it was creepy or how I found her chain on the exact path Mary Elizabeth had seen him jogging down that morning doesn't make him the killer." I knew common sense told us that it was quite obvious Bert Erickson killed Yaley Woodard, but it was the hard evidence and facts that would convict him.

"Then I guess we will still see you at the repast meeting." Betts sighed.

"Yes, ma'am, you will. And both of you keep looking into other possibilities because two other people have great motive." I carefully watched the GPS on the screen of my phone to find the entrance of the new distillery while I talked to them on speakerphone. "It's no secret killers like to throw detectives off the track, and it's possible Bert could've been set up. Just like the killer set up Joel."

"Very true." Abby's voice held intrigue. "I still think Bonnie Turner had a great motive. You've got money and greed."

My car followed the edge of the mountainous road. I kept a close eye on the edge. If I made the slightest wheel jerk, the car would go over the side and careen down the hill. There were so many caves, ledges, and edges in this part of the Daniel Boone National Forest that when people or cars fell off the road, it took rangers days to find them. I didn't want to be one of those statistics, so when I saw the huge wrought iron gates with fancy lettering and bourbon barrels welded in the middle, I was relieved to just drive up to the parking lot, turn off the car, and sit there for a moment to gather my wits.

I laid my head back on my headrest and closed my eyes. Queenie had always preached on taking deep breaths and long exhales to calm the nervous system. After the fourth one, I began to feel a little calmer.

"I'm telling you, I'm not going to rest until I get the land." The loud voice jarred my system back into overdrive.

My eyes flew open, my head flung forward, and my hands gripped the steering wheel.

"You get the deal done. Do you understand me?" Shane Holland was on the sidewalk in front of the wooden structure with his finger pointing at a woman with shoulder-length brown hair. She had on a brown pantsuit with a hot-pink scarf tied around her neck.

Her body was stiff, and I could make out the white on her knuckles from the grip she had on her briefcase.

"I understand that if you keep threatening me, I swear I will go before the board and tell them everything I know." The woman didn't back down from Shane. "So you better back off and give me time. This is how things operate in Normal, and you better get used to it."

I slid down into my seat when I noticed the woman was walking toward the parking lot, and I sure didn't want to be seen. I closed my eyes and held my breath as I heard her heels clicking past the car. It wasn't until I heard her start her car and drive away did I peek my eyes up over the dashboard to see if the coast was clear and Shane Holland had gone back into the building. I realized and felt it deep in my bones that there was something big going on here. I couldn't go see Shane Holland alone.

I reached over to the passenger seat and grabbed my phone.

"Hey, Abby," I whispered, still hunkered down in my seat. "I don't have time to talk now, but have you been on the Bourbon Trail Distillery's social media page?" My eyes glanced out the window, and I looked in the side mirror as the white SUV the woman was driving zoomed past my car.

"No, but I can." She must've been at the library now because I could hear her clicking on a keyboard. "What did you want to know?"

"I want to know if they are doing tours." I had an idea, but I knew I didn't want to do it alone.

"Yeah. It looks like when you click on the link to their website, it takes you to the page to book a tour." I heard more clicking.

"Do you want to take a tour?" I asked, knowing that if we could get inside on purpose, then we might have a shot at looking around.

"Are you telling me we are going to go undercover? Because if you are, I'm totally in." Abby's voice rose an octave.

"Yes. That's exactly what I'm saying." I pushed myself up to a sitting position, turned the car on, and threw it in Drive to get the heck out of there. "I think there's more to Shane Holland than fermenting alcohol, and it might not have anything to do with Yaley Woodard."

"The next available time for two people is tomorrow morning. Gosh, they are booked," Abby said. "Want me to take it?"

"Can you go tomorrow morning?" I questioned.

"Yes. One of the girls is back today from vacation. The page said the tour is an hour and a half, so I can use my lunch, plus a little extra time." Abby was all in, and I was relieved.

"Great. I'm getting the heck out of here." I didn't bother looking in the rearview mirror to see if Shane had come back out or if anyone noticed me.

"What on earth happened?" she asked.

"There was a woman here, and they were arguing. Apparently, he wants some land she has and was almost threatening her, but she gave it right back to him and threatened him with something he's hiding. Something about going in front of the board to tell them something." Everything that came out of my mouth sounded like code, and I didn't even understand it.

"Well, it looks like we've got some snooping to do." An evil laugh came out of Abby, but this time it didn't make me smile. It just made my stomach ping that something wasn't right.

"Now I wonder if Yaley Woodard knew something. A little too much of something, and it got her killed." If only I'd known just how much those words would come back to haunt me.

106

CHAPTER THIRTEEN

There was a little time to kill before my nail appointment, so I decided to park in front of Cute-icles and head over to Trails Coffee Shop to get me a much-needed jolt of caffeine. Now that I knew what Bert Erickson looked like, I could ask Sally Ann if she'd seen him. Or even got a glimpse of who was in Joel's truck now that she had some time to think about it.

Hank had always said, and it was true, that after a crime when he interviewed witnesses, he knew they were nervous and still a bit in shock. So he'd get an initial statement from them then go back a couple of days later after some of the shock had worn off and their minds had relaxed. He said that's when they could put more factual information together. So that's what I planned on doing with Sally Ann.

Now that I had more clues and timelines, and Joel was not the number one suspect, though Hank would never say Joel was completely off the hook, maybe Sally Ann had a little more time to process and think. Even the slightest memory might help.

"Hey there." Gert Hobson was behind the counter of the Trails Coffee Shop, pushing all sorts of buttons and jiggling the small handle on one of her fancy coffee machines. "I just made a fresh pot of coffee.

Help yourself." She raised her head toward the steaming pot of coffee at the far end of the counter.

"Look at your wall," I gasped when I noticed the living wall the fancy architect Gert had hired to create using plants, flowers, and greenery local to the Daniel Boone National Forest. It was pretty neat. "The wildflowers are so amazing this time of the year."

The pops of purples, blues, yellows, reds, and oranges really stood out against the wall of the coffee shop. It was just one of the cool features Gert had in her shop. She used a mix of café tables, along with long farm tables for her customers. In the middle of each one, she had repurposed old bourbon barrel lids and made really cool lazy Susans out of them.

Each lazy Susan was a home for the little containers of various condiments that coffee shop customers needed to doctor up their coffees the way they wanted.

Gert had taken her shop to a whole 'nother level, and it was a true experience to come to have a cup of coffee.

While she made a customer's fancy coffee, my phone chirped a text, and by the sound, I knew it was Abby. I made my cup and sat down at one of the small café tables to see what Abby had texted me.

"Well darn." Disappointment fell over me when I read Abby's text.

"You okay?" Gert moseyed over but not without stopping at the tables along the way and straightening up something.

"Abby and I were going to go to the new Bourbon Trail Distillery for a tour tomorrow, and now she has to work at the library." I frowned and watched Gert pull out the chair across from me and sit down.

Gert let out a big yawn. "I'm sorry. It's been crazy busy here with all the ruckus going on. So many people coming in to talk about the body you found."

"Yeah. That." I rolled my eyes. "I'm glad your business is doing good, but I've had so many cancellations that I'm worried."

"You'll be fine. Hank will get this all solved, and life will go back to normal. Campers will be itching to get back to living out in the park for a week or two. But if you want to see the distillery, I've got to pick up some barrel lids Shane Holland sold me." Gert waved to a customer who walked in the door. One of her baristas stepped up to help him, so Gert stayed with me.

"Really?" I studied whether I should tell her exactly why I was going to the distillery but decided not to. "When?"

"I can go whenever." She shrugged. "I've got an employee here all the time, now that I'm getting the royalties from Moonbucks."

"That's great, Gert." I couldn't help but remembering how devastating it was that Gert's special coffee blend recipe had been stolen by the owner of the national coffee chain Moonbucks, but now that it was all worked out, she seemed to have come out on the other side of things.

"How is Joel?" she asked, shifting her eyes to the door. I glanced back to see what caught her attention.

"We can ask him." I raised my hand in the air when he saw me. "Hey. I was going to check on you today."

Joel peeled off his cap and held it to his chest.

"I can't ever thank you enough for calling that lawyer. Now I just need to find out what happened to Yaley and my truck." His eyes dipped at the corners.

"You want your usual?" Gert asked Joel. She stood up and gave him her seat.

"I don't want to take your seat." He was so polite.

"I've got to get to work. You sit and relax. I'll grab your favorite." Gert stood up and hugged Joel. He clasped on to her a little. She patted him. "It's all going to be okay."

"You've got me." I winked and offered him a friendly smile. "How are you?" I asked when he sat down.

"Honestly?" He drummed his fingers on the table. There was fresh grease under his nails. "Tired. Confused. Sad. Angry. Tired. Worried."

His facial expressions changed with every word he said.

"I've been trying to keep busy at the shop, but no one wants to bring their car to a killer." He looked down at his fingers. "Gosh. I should go wash my hands."

"Nah. Nobody cares." I reached across the table and patted his hands. "Listen, I want to help you. Hank wants me to help you. But I need to know exactly what happened that morning."

"It really started the night before. I picked her up to go to the Red Barn for supper. It was our three-month dating anniversary." There was a slight smile on his lips, and a sparkle in his eyes. I could picture their supper at the fancy restaurant.

It's hard to imagine an old barn could be turned into the most romantic restaurant you'd ever seen. But it was. It was also the most expensive place to eat in Normal, so I knew if Joel had taken her there, it was special.

"She looked so pretty. She had on a blue dress and her hair fixed up. Normally, she wore what she'd worn to work, but it was special. Little did I realize she was going to break up with me." His voice cracked.

"Did she break up with you at the Red Barn?" I wondered why she broke up with him and would ask if he didn't tell me.

"No. We had supper, and I took her back to my place. It was a nice night. We got a beer and sat outside. She told me about the financial trouble her and her brother had gotten into a few years back." He pulled his hands out from under mine when Gert brought over the biggest and craziest coffee concoction I'd ever seen.

"Here you go." Gert set it down in front of him. "I put on extra whip." She patted his back before she headed back to the counter.

"What on earth is that?" I couldn't take my eyes off of it. Not only was it a cream color and served in a large mason jar, but there was a pile of whipped cream with chocolate chips to finish it off on top.

"I like a lot of protein in my diet, so Gert keeps a special cold brew blend and some protein powder called 'Cookie Bar' here for me." He picked it up and took a sip, whipped cream getting all over his lips. "She uses a base of vanilla protein powder with ice and the cold brew, along with some almond milk and a couple scoops of the protein powder. It's amazin'. Want to try?"

"I think I'll stick to my black coffee." I watched him take more sips of the drink.

"Don't knock it 'til you try it, May-bell-ine." It was good to hear him tease.

"When she was telling you about her brother, was she talking about how she funneled all the tourists' accommodations to her brother's properties first?" I asked.

"Yeah. I would ask how you know about it, but I'm figuring you've been doing your homework while Hank held me down at the jail." He glanced over the top of the whipped cream.

"Yeah. If you think your business is bad, imagine how many cancellations I've gotten since she was found in my dumpster." I sucked in a deep breath. "So do you understand the more information you can give me will not only help you, but help me find the real killer?"

"I do. It's just so hard. But she said when her brother approached her about it, she didn't see any problem with it. And I believe her. I think she just wanted to help out her brother and didn't see any harm in giving him business. The customers didn't always pick his rentals. Yaley had given them the option. Then Bonnie Turner got wind, and since some of her property was usually the first to go since it had better locations, she realized what was going on. She brought all those charges against them until they finally settled with her." He shook his head with a look of disgust on his face.

"How much did they have to pay Bonnie?" I questioned and knew I had to go see Bonnie too.

"Ummm...you know the land where that new distillery is located?" He must've seen the shocked look on my face. If I knew where he was going with this, it was a clear connection between Shane Holland, Bonnie Turner, and Yaley that would give a solid motive. "Apparently, you do. Well, all that land was Yaley and Ted's. They'd inherited it, and it was what Bonnie wanted instead of a cash settlement because it was all Yaley and Ted had. Instead of trying to sell it themselves to get the money to pay off the settlement, they turned the property over to Bonnie. She ended up doing an investment in the distillery."

Stunned, I was literally sick to my stomach.

"Mae?" His brows furrowed. "You okay?"

"I'm fine." I brought myself out of my thoughts, where I was trying to piece together Bonnie and Shane. "If she was planning on breaking up with you, why would she tell you all this?"

"That's what was so weird. While she was telling me, she got a phone call from Ted. He wanted to know when he should expect her home, and she told him we were talking and not sure. That's when it all changed. She walked away from me and finished the call where I couldn't hear her. She came back, and it was like a switch turned off. She said it was time for her to go home and took off to the truck." Sadness swept across his face. He gulped. "I begged her to tell me what happened while she gave me the cold shoulder back to her place. She turned and told me she needed to break up. I was sick. I pulled the truck over and just had to sit there. She ended up telling me to go back to my house."

He paused. He cupped his hands around the fancy cold brew coffee and took a few deep swallows. When he looked up at me, there were tears in his eyes.

"I'm sorry," he apologized.

"Don't you dare apologize. You loved her." I tried not to hurry him, but my nail appointment was soon, and now more than ever, I needed to find out who was in Joel's truck and took Yaley.

"Yeah. I didn't know until that moment, and I told her." His lip curled with the memory. "She started to cry. She spent the better part of the night crying and saying how her life since she moved to Normal had been anything but normal. Honestly, we sat there all night while she cried and talked all sorts of gibberish. She talked about how she got demoted from the real estate side after Bonnie got her claws in them and that got her demoted at the Sierra Club to doing tours, which she doesn't like, but she did it for a paycheck. I still haven't made sense of it all. Every day I remember something."

"You do know that you might remember something that can help solve her murder, right?" I told him. "Whatever you remember, write it down. I know some things might sound insignificant to you, but in the grand scheme, it could be a tiny piece of the puzzle to help solve her murder."

"Yeah. I try to." He wasn't committed to writing it down, which didn't surprise me. "But the sun was coming up over the pond at my place, and she glanced over at me. Told me she was sorry and that she needed to go home to get ready for work."

"Anything strange when you did that? Her brother? Anyone follow you?" I asked him.

"Not that I saw. But I wasn't paying attention to anything but her. I grabbed her purse off the kitchen table and carried it to the truck. She got in, and I drove her to her house. She took her purse and told me to give her some space. I was happy after that. It was a little window of hope. Instead of going home, I went to Steve's junkyard, dropped off my truck, and picked up his car." He swirled the mason jar, swishing around the last bit of his drink before he finished it off. "I didn't see Steve. I didn't talk to Steve. We've got an understanding that I drop off my truck, and when I pick my truck up, I leave his car right there, finished."

"That's the last time you saw your truck?" I asked.

"Yep. Bobby Ray was off that morning. I still had the car, but Hank said I could've gone back and gotten my truck since I didn't have an alibi." He took a deep breath.

"What about the flowers? Did you send those to her?" Though I knew he probably didn't, I still wanted to know how he got her call to meet him at the amphitheater.

"Flowers? What flowers?" He tilted his head and lowered his eyes.

"Someone sent her flowers from Sweet Smell Flower Shop, and it said, 'Meet me for lunch at the amphitheater.' According to Diane at the Sierra Club, Yaley got excited and thought it was you. That's when she texted to meet you."

He ran his hand along his head. Fear and worry tugged as his jaw tensed.

"Are you telling me that someone knew we got into a fight and that they used me to kill her?" His nostrils flared. The anger was building up inside of him as his chest heaved up and down.

"I think someone stole your truck, sent her flowers to ask to meet at the amphitheater, and picked her up in your truck. I'm not sure if they knew you had a fight or broke up, but I do know that when your truck pulled up to the sidewalk, she hesitated before she got in." I watched Joel crumple before my eyes, and my heart tore into a million pieces. "Joel. I'm sorry. I told you this was going to be hard, but I need answers."

"I'm gonna find the son-of-a—" He talked through clenched teeth.

"Joel." I put my hand up to stop him. "You getting revenge on someone right now isn't going to help anyone's case. You're still a suspect, and until I can find answers, you will remain low-key." I gave him a good hard stare. "Do you understand me?"

"Loud and clear." He raised his chin in the air and stared down his nose at me. "I won't rest until her killer is brought to justice. And I'm gonna write down things as you said."

"Good. Now, I'm going to get my nails done because Sally Ann told me about how Yaley got into the truck. So she's a witness to that, and I'm going to try to get some more information from her." I remembered the necklace. "Before I forget, what can you tell me about Yaley's necklace?"

He smiled.

"I loved those little hearts. I even kissed them around her neck a few times. I can hear her giggle now, telling me how it tickled her." He smiled, then grew serious. "What about it?"

"She didn't have it on when I found her, but I did read on the flyer how she never took it off. Then today after I got a tip about Bert Erickson…" I stopped talking when I saw his face flush. "Do you know Bert?"

"I know he bugged the crap out of her. She said that night how she hated doing tours because this one creepy guy always found out her tour schedule and was always there. He even showed up at her house where Ted had to threaten him." Everything Joel was telling me was solidifying how much of a stalker Bert was to Yaley.

"Well, he was seen at The Cookie Crumble when you and Yaley were there that morning." I tried to read Joel's blank stare, but it was as if he'd turned into a robot. "I decided to walk the trail he runs, and I found the heart chain. Not the pendant but the chain."

"I'll kill him, Mae." His words were slow and monotone. It sent a sheer fright down to the middle of my bones.

"No. He's in custody now. Let Hank do his job." I stood up because I had to go to my appointment at Cute-icles. "Your job is to remember anything Yaley said to you when she was upset and write it down. Anything."

He nodded. I gave him one more hug before I headed out the door.

I took my phone out of my bag and called Hank.

"This Bert guy is unbelievable," Hank answered without a hello. "He thinks it's normal to have a tour guide you like and only go on those tours, not caring where the tour takes you."

"I had an interesting conversation with Joel over coffee at Trails." I quickly told Hank about Joel's last night with Yaley, and we compared notes.

The gist of it was about the same, only he wasn't as emotional with Hank's interview in jail. Hank was happy that Joel agreed to write down anything he remembered, which went back to Hank's theory about how victims remembered things a few days after the shock had worn off. Joel was no different.

"Did you follow up with Ted Woodard?" I asked Hank.

"Yeah. His wife and kids were with him all night. He runs his rental business out of their home, so it was easy to trace his steps. He was actually meeting with a tourist all day. They are renting for the entire summer, so they were going around to properties all day. And he had receipts for a two-hour lunch with them at the Red Barn. He's clear."

"Did you know the Woodards settled with Bonnie Turner by giving her the land where the Bourbon Trail Distillery is built?" I questioned.

"We got that news today when Ted asked if we thought Bonnie Turner could be involved." Hank was on top of things. "And the finger-prints on the purse and necklace don't match with Bert Erickson."

"What?" I sucked in a deep breath of disappointment and turned around. I glanced at the display window of Cute-icles and caught Helen Pyle's eye. I tried to quickly turn back around and not make eye contact, but it was too late.

She hurried out the door of the pale-yellow cottage-style home with the cute gingerbread latticework along the top.

"I see you!" she hollered and rushed down the steps to the sidewalk before reaching the gate to the fenced-in yard. Her bejeweled nails glistened in the sunshine when she flipped the lock on the gate to open it.

"You're late. Get in here. We are full up." She huffed and puffed under her mile-high orange hairdo. The old-fashioned wooden sign with the shop's name on it and a spotlight below it caught her attention for a moment. She ran her hand along the sparkly painted name and scowled when she noticed some of it was peeling, muttering something under her breath.

Glitter and big hair had never gone out of style in Normal.

"Listen, he was obsessed with her," I whispered into the phone so Helen's big ears didn't hear me, even though her beady eyes were now snapping my way. "He even showed up at her house."

"Yes. Ted told me, Mae. You just listen for more gossip, and call me when you get them nails all done up with glitter and who knows what else Sally Ann is going to do to you now that she's got you exactly where she wants you," he joked before we said our goodbyes.

Only it wasn't a joke. Sally Ann gets one chance every six months to do something to me. Usually, I let her trim my hair or maybe straighten it, but it never stopped her from begging me to let her do more, and that meant adding a little sparkle.

"What are you waiting on, Mae?" Helen groaned at the gate, her foot keeping it open.

"I had to talk to Hank." I sighed and walked in the gate. "You know men. They don't know what we go through for beauty."

"Mae West, I know I'm around all these chemicals all day long, making sure all the ladies, and some gentlemen, keep looking good, but it hasn't made me stupid."

Confused, I followed her along the walk, up the steps, and into the shop.

"I've got supersonic ears." She tapped her ears with her long jeweled fingernails before she shoved me down into the chair and plunged my fingers into a warm bowl of water with marbles at the bottom. "And I know you were talking about that girl we saw get in Joel Grassle's truck before whoever it was stole off with her and…" Helen dragged her finger across her neck.

"We saw?" I questioned Helen. The nail light on the table shined, creating an eerie glow on her face.

"Yes. We. We were all sitting here talking, and we heard Joel drive up because Lord knows it sounds like a tornado whipping through when he drives through town." She grabbed a towel from underneath the manicure table and pulled one of my hands out, placed it in the towel, and patted it dry. "I even said there should be some sort of ordinance against letting your muffler get so bad."

She set that hand aside and took the other one out of the water, repeating the same technique.

"Where's Sally Ann?" I asked. "I had an appointment with her."

"Oh, she had to go to the church. They are doing a repast supper for poor Yaley, so I sent her so we could be represented." She opened the top drawer and took out a fingernail file.

"I thought it wasn't until a couple of hours from now." I wasn't used to helping make repast dinners, so I could've been entirely wrong.

"You're right." Helen put on her reader glasses before she picked up my hand to start grinding away on the nails. "But it's the pre-coffee chat where I like to show everyone how we are a part of the community, and care takes place before the actual cooking. I mean," she looked up over the rim of the bejeweled readers at me, "some folks come to drop off the uncooked food, stay for some coffee chat, and then the ladies of the church spend the rest of the day cooking the meals brought in. You know."

I didn't know, but the picture was becoming increasingly clear.

Helen was telling me they were gossiping right now, and I was missing it.

"You know what." I peeled my hand out of hers. "I forgot. I'm going to be raking the lake at Happy Trails today. You know." I waved my hand in the air. "Gotta get up all that moss before the new season campers come tomorrow."

"You aren't getting a manicure?" She drew back, and her shoulder collapsed, her hands gripped the nail file. "Honey, those nails are wretched."

"Yeah, well, you should see them after I get all that moss up under them." I stood up and threw my crossbody bag around me. "Before I go, did you see who was driving Joel's truck?"

"Obviously, we all thought it was Joel, but then earlier today, Violet Rhinehammer was in here, getting her hair colored, and she said someone stole Joel's car." Helen's eyes drifted past my shoulder, and she looked out the window. "No wonder the poor girl hesitated."

"You noticed Yaley hesitate?" I knew Sally Ann had said the same thing, but I needed to be clear on what Helen saw with her own eyes.

"Heavens, yes. I know the street out there past our front sign and all, but when your attention is on that god-awful muffler sound and you see someone as cute as Yaley Woodard go up and look in, back away, and walk up again before finally getting in, then you know she hesitated."

"And you didn't look at the driver?" I asked.

"Why would I need to look at the driver when I knew whose car it was?" She inhaled and let out a long sigh. "Though now I wish I had."

"Thanks, Helen," I said over my shoulder on the way out of the salon. "I'm sorry for the confusion."

I hurried down the walk and out the gate.

"Whoa!" Skip Toliver twirled around me with a fancy coffee in his hand. He looked like a typical hiker. He was wearing a plaid, long-sleeved shirt tucked into a pair of hunter-green shorts with tall brown socks ending in a pair of hiking boots all tied up. The loose sandy-blond curls that fell around his head made me swoon with jealousy. I ran my hand down my hair and, for one second, thought I should turn around and run back into Cute-icles. "What's the hurry?" he asked.

"I'm going to be late for the gossip at the repast cooking for Yaley Woodard." My mouth watered at the sight of his cold brew drink. "That looks good."

"Iced mocha." He held it out in front of him. "Want a sip?"

"No thanks, but I see your whitewater rafting is going good." I had a second I could catch up with him. Maybe he had some information on the Sierra Club and where his tours stood. "I was on the other side of the river near the Milkery, and I heard your group going down the rapids. They were having so much fun."

"Yeah. It's a blast." He grinned. "Say, I need to get you out there. You like living on the edge with all your investigations."

"Thanks, but I'm not one for real danger where I'm deliberately putting my life on the line." I thought it was funny how everyone in Normal was starting to see me as some sort of sleuth. "Speaking of sleuthing, did you see anyone strange on the trails the days between the time Yaley Woodard went missing?"

"Almost all the people I see daily are people I don't know." He took a big suck on his straw. "I see you most regularly during the warmer seasons. Other than that…" He shrugged. "Do I need to keep my eye out?"

"I think Yaley's killer dumped her necklace on the trail." It sounded crazy when I said it out loud. It made no sense whatsoever. "I think the killer was keeping an eye on Yaley. They somehow stole Joel's truck. Whoever it was pulled up right here, and when she hesitated to get in, the killer somehow sweet-talked her into the truck."

"What?" Skip looked at me as if I was nuts.

"Someone stole Joel's truck, and whoever stole it picked up Yaley here. It was the last time she was seen." I looked at the road and wondered how Yaley felt that afternoon, standing there.

"Did anyone see the truck?" he asked.

"Yes. The ladies in the salon." I pointed to Cute-icles behind me.

"But they didn't think too much because the truck was Joel's, and they had no idea it was stolen."

"That's too bad. When she didn't show up to give me the tour dates, I figured she decided not to put me on the schedule." Skip had such a laid-back attitude.

Skip had grown up around here, and he loved to hike and take his time. I admired his no-worries kind of attitude. When he'd opened the canoe and whitewater rafting attraction, he'd done all the legwork and had a lot of friends help him get it going. I also made sure I advertised it because it was just a quick hike down the Red Fox Trail and perfect for my guests.

"There's a lady named Diane in the Sierra Club office that helped me when I went in the other day," I told him. "You might want to give her a call if you've not heard about tours. The season does start this weekend."

"Yeah, I'll do that," he said nonchalantly as though he was just agreeing with me to appease me.

"I've got to get going to the repast. I'll hike down later with Fifi." We said our goodbyes.

* * *

THE NORMAL BAPTIST Church undercroft was a large room with old tile flooring. Queenie French rented the room from the church so she could hold her Jazzercise classes down there. According to her, that's where most small towns held their classes. It didn't seem to bother her any.

But today, her afternoon classes were canceled, and overhearing her talking to the ladies I didn't know, they were all here to help with Yaley's repast supper. I found them in the kitchen in the far back of the room.

"You're early." Betts greeted me with a smile. "You okay?" she asked as Queenie hurried over.

I nodded for them to follow me out of the kitchen and into a vacant area of the undercroft so I could tell them all about Bert Erickson.

"Then we have our killer." Queenie nodded with wide eyes.

"No." I shook my head. "His fingerprints don't match the prints found on Yaley's necklace or her purse. I'm afraid we are back to Bonnie Turner and Shane Holland." I looked over my shoulder to make sure we were still alone when I noticed a woman walking past us. A woman with a hot-pink scarf tied around her neck.

My eyes grew, my hands got clammy, and my armpits began to sweat. When she walked past with her eyes fixed on mine, my heart beat so fast that I actually gasped to make sure I was getting air.

"Are you okay?" Betts touched my arm.

"I'm...ahem"—I cleared my throat—"I'm fine."

"You went pale." Betts turned her head to see where my attention had gone. "That's Bonnie," Betts gasped. "What is she doing here?"

"Bonnie Turner?" I questioned, hardly able to choke down the fact that Bonnie Turner was the woman I'd seen with Shane Holland in front of the Bourbon Trail Distillery. The woman who had practically threatened Shane with some big secret.

Chills started from the tips of my toes and went up to the tips of my fingers.

"Alright," Queenie took me by the arms, "there's something wrong. You've got goose bumps all over your arms, and it's hotter than blue blazes in here."

"Excuse me," Bonnie Turner interrupted us. "Hi, Betts. I got a message from the prayer chain that everyone would be here to make the repast food for our sweet Yaley Woodard. Shame." She tsk-tsked and looked at me. A smile curled up her lips. "I've brought a gift card from the grocery, so you can get whatever you need since I don't have time to cook." She clasped her hands in front of her and turned to me. Her brown hair swung around her shoulder. "Do I know you?" she asked me directly.

"I don't think so." I shrugged Queenie off of me and stood there, looking into what could possibly be a killer's eyes.

"No." Her eyes narrowed, one more than the other. "I know you from somewhere."

"Maybe one of the campground monthly parties." Betts quickly nodded. I could tell she was trying to make light of the situation because Betts knew me well enough to know I was acting funny, and I'd just asked who Bonnie was. "Where are my manners? Bonnie Turner, this is Mae West."

"The Mae West who got the key to the city a year or so ago for her contribution to the economy here in Normal." Queenie threw in her two cents.

"Nice to meet you." I put my hand out to shake, only she didn't take it. She simply looked down at it then drew her eyes back up to meet mine.

"Hmmm." A smile curled on her face. She looked between Betts and Queenie. "Do you two mind if I have a word with Ms. West alone?"

Betts and Queenie looked at me.

"Sure, it's fine," I assured them with an upbeat tone, acting as if it was no big deal.

There was an uncomfortable silence between us while Betts and Queenie moved away. Queenie had positioned herself in the kitchen so she had direct visual on me.

"Do you work at the Sierra Club?" I questioned. "Maybe that's where I know you since your group promotes the campground as a place to stay."

"No." She quickly shot me down. "I don't know what you want, but I know you were in the parking lot of the distillery"—she looked down at her watch—"just a few hours ago, and you might've thought you weren't seen, but I hate to tell you that your hair is much higher than the door of that little car you drive. When I walked back to my car, I could see you hunkered down out of the corner of my eye."

"Oh." I had nothing to say to that. "I-I—"

"Don't try to make up any excuses. I asked around when I was back at the office, and plenty of people know who you are and what you drive, so it was pretty easy for people to tell me exactly who you are and how much you love to help your boyfriend out." She shoved her hands into the pockets of the brown pantsuit's trousers. "I know you were also at the office talking to Diane, so I'm warning you that if you don't stop snooping around, you'll regret it." She took one step closer to me and whispered directly into my ear, "I promise you'll regret it."

I tried not to show any emotion when Bonnie took a step back, because I could feel her eyes on me. I wasn't going to give her any satisfaction in believing she'd gotten to me.

The heels of her shoes clicked as she walked across the old tile floor. It wasn't until I heard the latch of the door close after she'd left that I stopped holding my breath.

I didn't stay around long enough to see what else Bonnie Turner had to say to me. Betts and Queenie were shell-shocked at how Bonnie Turner had threatened me. They told me I needed to tell Hank.

"She said that to you?" Hank asked, questioning the validity of my story.

"Yes. She clearly knew I was there, and she obviously knows that I know something about her involvement with Yaley's murder." I had gone to my car to leave the church so I could go back to the campground where I would get a much-needed break from all that had happened today. My brain wasn't going to be able to hold much more.

I glanced around the parking lot to see if I could spot the white SUV I'd seen Bonnie get in at the distillery, but it wasn't there. She must've peeled right on out of there.

"Now you're speculating, but I don't like the fact she said you'd regret it." There was a sudden chill in his words. "I don't have reason to bring either of them in on the charges with Yaley, but I could stop by the Sierra Club office and have a little chat. I could question her again on the lawsuit she'd filed against the Woodards, but according to Ted, that's all over with."

"I don't know. Maybe Yaley knew something about whatever it was that Shane and Bonnie were talking about, and they killed her." I gulped down the words. They tasted really bitter going down. "There's something in my gut that tells me there's more to it than Ted or Bonnie has told you."

"I think you're right." Hank's sigh came through the phone loud and clear.

"Hey, Gert Hobson is calling me. I need to take it." I put the keys in the ignition. "What is your plan? Because I'm going home."

"I am going to go by the Sierra Club office, and then I'll be home after that for a quick bite to eat."

Hank wasn't fooling me.

First off, he never came home to eat during an investigation. Secondly, I knew he wanted to get eyes on me after I'd been threatened to make sure I was okay. That's the kind of guy Hank was. He might not be the door-holding, pulling-out-the-dinner-table-chair southern gentleman, but he was the man who would make sure I was safe, taken care of, and loved. That's why I loved him so much.

"Hey, Gert," I answered after Hank and I said goodbye.

"Where are you?" she asked.

"I'm sitting in the parking lot of the Normal Baptist Church." I felt my lungs expand. It was nice to finally have a big, deep breath now that Bonnie was long gone.

"I was going to head on out to the distillery to pick up those bourbon barrel lids. Do you want to come?" Gert asked.

Though it was so tempting to tell her no, go home to crawl in bed, and forget the day and how I was literally threatened, I knew I wasn't going to let anyone, not even Bonnie Turner, get to me.

"Sure. I'd love to," I blurted out and had already put the car in gear, driving straight out on the country road to the Bourbon Trail Distillery.

CHAPTER FOURTEEN

Gert and I had agreed to meet there because she was going to go home after she picked up the lids, and I was going to go back to the campground where I wanted to check on Dottie and cook her and Hank some supper.

I owed Dottie a big thank-you for holding down the campground the past couple of days. And I wanted to know what Hank said to Bonnie.

If he even saw Bonnie, because it looked like her white SUV was parked in the distillery parking lot. After seeing her car, I had a second where I almost turned the car around because I sure didn't want Bonnie to see me at the distillery and make her threat come true. But then I decided it might be good for her to see that I'm not going to take anything from her and that her words were just puffs of air that meant nothing to me.

There was a toot of a car horn that made me jerk my head up to look in the rearview mirror. Gert had pulled up and was waving at me. I waved back, turned my car off, and grabbed my hobo bag from the passenger seat before I got out to meet her.

"You're going to love this place." Gert was excited to share the experience. Even her walk had a sunny cheerfulness. "I bet Shane gives you a bottle to take home with you. You two might even come up with a basket collaboration. I don't think you could put him in the hospitality room since you don't have a liquor license."

"Aren't you the marketer for them?" I joked, though it was a nice idea for one of the many baskets. I didn't sell wine either, but the Honeymoon Basket and the Bridal Baskets all had the option. The men would love the bourbon, and I could also promote the distillery tour.

Too bad Shane Holland might be going to jail—if not for the murder of Yaley Woodard, then maybe for whatever it was Bonnie Turner held over his head.

"They have all sorts of souvenirs too." Gert grabbed the handle of the large glass entrance door.

She was right. The distillery entrance opened up into a gift shop that had the Bourbon Trail Distillery logo on every single piece of merchandise. They had posters, shirts, koozies, shot glasses, hats, caps, sunglasses, bottle openers, magnets. You name it, they had it. Then there was the display of the various bourbons and labels. There were interactive television screens where you could even make your own label for them to put on a bottle of their bourbon.

There was a free Sierra Club magazine sitting in one of the display wire racks with this season's date on it. I grabbed it, wondering when they distributed these and if my ad was in there.

While Gert continued to give me her verbal tour, I gave her a lot of uh-huhs, mm-hmms, and head nods, but my attention was on flipping through the magazine to find my ad that I paid for months ago. When I got to the two-page spread in the middle, the Bourbon Trail Distillery was bigger and brighter than the sun shining over Normal this very minute.

This didn't make sense. I'd heard about Yaley not giving him the ad and how his paperwork wasn't turned in on time. No exceptions—wasn't that what Queenie had told me and the rest of the Laundry Club ladies?

"Hey there, Shane." Gert's smile grew bigger. "This is my friend, Mae. She'd love a tour."

Shane looked at me. There still wasn't a hair out of place since I'd seen him making bourbon balls with Ty Randal at the Normal Diner. His well-groomed eyebrows framed his eyes perfectly. The Bourbon Trail Distillery shirt he wore was tight enough to show off his biceps and chest.

"I saw you at the diner." He flashed a smile that probably made women swoon.

Not me. I wasn't falling for his model charm. *Killer. Secret keeper.* My thoughts pictured his hands fastening around Yaley's neck, her flailing to fight him off, and his hand ripping the chain off her neck.

"Yeah. Your bourbon balls were good." I figured I'd be nice until I could get some questions out.

"Thanks. We're glad we finally got the place opened up. I thought we were going to have to wait until the fall season, but we made it in with the paperwork right in the nick of time." He nodded and looked between me and Gert. "You're going to love the lids I've saved."

He motioned for us to follow him through another door. I folded the magazine in half and put it in my back pocket, hoping for a good time to bring it out and ask Shane about it.

I let Gert go ahead of me so I could get my bearings as we walked around the conveyor belt of glass bottles as they went under the machine that filled them with the gold-brown liquid Kentucky was known for. It was really fascinating to see, but I didn't want to get too caught up in the pomp and circumstance and let my guard down in case we ran into Bonnie Turner.

"The lids I have for you were just pried off yesterday. In fact, they are still sitting on the barrels themselves." He shook a finger at Gert. "You're going to get an up close and personal view of the fermenting process. Plus, your lids are going to smell so good."

Shane Holland didn't need the Sierra Club to help sell his tours. He was a one-man pony show. I found myself getting lost in his excitement. I found my awe soared when he opened the door to another room, and there were bourbon barrels by the hundreds that were lying on their side and stacked up to the ceiling in rows and rows.

"These are barrels that haven't aged." He ran his hand down the barrels as we walked down the row. "They are also for sale."

"For sale?" Gert asked.

"Yep. You can buy this barrel here, and when it's ready to be opened, tapped, whatever you want to call it, we would have you come here and do the honors. Bring friends. Have a party. Drink your bourbon from your barrel. Then we'd make you bottles to take home with your very own designed label, and you also get to keep the barrel." He had me inches away from telling him I'd buy one. "But these here"—he stopped at three barrels standing up—"are the three lids you get to take with you."

"Exciting." Gert's brows rose then fell. "The ones I'd bought for Trails Coffee Shop were from antique stores, and a couple a few friends had. I'm really excited to come here and support you so I can tell everyone who comes in and sits at the tables with your lids that I got them from our *local* bourbon distillery and send them here for a tour."

"Do you have any brochures I can leave at the campground?" I found myself wanting to help him out.

"You're the campground owner I've been hearing so much about." He put the two together.

"I hope it's been good." I shrugged and realized I just blew my cover. "Mae West. I'm surprised Ty didn't tell you who I was."

"He might've, but we were so busy making those orders of bourbon balls. I needed to sell him on buying my bourbon, so I was laser focused." He rubbed his hands together before he pulled off the lid, flipping it over to let Gert take a smell.

"Goodness, it smells so fresh," Gert gushed.

He offered me a whiff. I took one, but I really wasn't sure what I was trying to smell for.

"I'm not a big bourbon drinker, but it's nice. So do you have some brochures to give me?" I questioned. "I'm guessing Yaley Woodard was your representative, too, since she did most businesses in Normal."

I should've told Gert why I wanted to come because, by the look on her face, I'd completely embarrassed her.

"Yaley wouldn't take my business. She claimed I didn't go through the proper channels and get my paperwork in on time, but as you can see, I don't need her little magazine." His words made my stomach crawl.

"Really?" I pulled the magazine out of my back pocket and flipped right to the middle, holding out the two-page spread to him and Gert. "And you didn't swindle her and Ted out of this land by making some sort of deal with Bonnie Turner, who just so happened to drop the lawsuit because the Woodards settled with her by giving her the land where she probably turned around and sold it to you. And I'm figuring Bonnie Turner could be brought up on extortion charges if Ted Woodard wants to make that claim."

"Mae," Gert gasped. "I'm sorry, Shane. We will just take the lids and be going."

"It looks like we've got ourselves a little sleuth here." He grinned, and it reached his eyes, curling them up at the edges. He appeared to be enjoying toying with me. "I guess you could say that I took every opportunity I could to open my distillery, and by the looks of it, I'm going to surpass any type of monetary contribution your little campground made to the economy of Normal." He put his hand on the edges of the next bourbon barrel lid. "I'm guessing you don't like competition, Ms. West."

He lifted the lid up over his head, and just as he did, a hand popped out and draped over the edge of the barrel. A pink scarf entwined around the fingers told me exactly who was in the barrel.

Just like that, my second suspect, Bonnie Turner, was now the second victim.

CHAPTER FIFTEEN

"Get her out of here." Shane Holland shot a look of death at me as he paced back and forth while Hank tried to question me, Shane, and Gert.

"Me?" I pointed to myself and curled up onto my toes. "What about you?" I shoved my finger at him. "You're the one with motive to have killed both Yaley and Bonnie. I heard you tell Bonnie to get the deal done. What deal were you talking about?" I kept throwing questions at him. "What about her threatening to go before the board to tell your secret? Tell Hank what your secret is. You killed Bonnie to shut her up."

"Mae." Hank put his hand on me, and I jerked away.

"Not to mention that Bonnie just so happened to threaten me at the church of all places!" My voice grew louder as I kept spewing out everything I knew. "She told me I'd regret it, but it looks like she regretted something. What was she holding over your head, Shane?"

"She's insane." Shane pointed to me and talked to Hank. "I'm not saying another word until I have my lawyer present. And I certainly want her off my property. That's my right, and I want her gone. Now!"

"Killers don't have rights," I spat back.

"Okay, Mae, enough." Hank raised his chin for the sheriff's deputy to take Shane inside while Hank took me and Gert over to our cars.

130

Gert was still in a state of shock. Her hands hung by her side, and her head was down. Her shoulders were slumped.

"Hank, you have to take him in. Come on." I threw my hands up in the air.

"This." He dragged the toe of his shoe on the parking lot concrete. "This is the line I've drawn, and you've crossed it. You are done. You get in your car and go home." I opened my mouth. "Ah." He pointed to my car. "Go home. I'll see you later."

"Fine." I wasn't fine. I wanted to see Shane Holland in handcuffs. I wanted to see Bonnie Turner in handcuffs, too, but the gurney carrying her body under a sheet was all I was going to see.

Instead of doing what Hank had asked us to do, Gert and I sat in my car and watched Colonel load the gurney into the back of the hearse just like I'd watched him do with Yaley a couple of days ago.

There was a silence that hung between me and Gert. Hank had gone into the distillery.

"I had no idea." Gert looked over at me, stunned. "I thought this whole time he was just a nice young man, who really wanted to start a legitimate business."

"I don't think he set out with extortion in his business plan, but I do think that he got so wrapped up in wanting to start his business that he was grasping at whatever he could to get it going, and if that meant Bonnie Turner was involved..." I shook my head. "I just can't believe how Yaley was caught up in all of this and how—"

"Look," Gert interrupted and pointed out the window at the deputy, who was bringing Shane out of the distillery in handcuffs.

Hank walked out, and like a magnet, he looked over at me and Gert. He walked over.

"He doesn't look happy." Gert made a very good observation.

"Yeah. He's not. He wanted us to leave." I rolled down the window when he walked up.

"Ladies." Hank bent down and looked in the window. "I thought I told you two to go home."

"You did, but I needed to see what was going to happen with Shane."

How could Hank think I was going to leave now? "You know I had to see it through."

"If it makes you feel any better, we were already onto the scheme Shane and Bonnie had pulled on the Woodards, only it's not completely illegal. Maybe immoral, but not illegal." Hank didn't make it out as if it was too big of a deal. "When we questioned Bonnie about her relationship with Yaley, she told us about the argument between Yaley and Shane. How he'd threatened her. Bonnie didn't tell us about the business arrangement she and Shane had."

"What was that?" Gert asked.

"Apparently, Shane and Bonnie were joint owners of the distillery. Bonnie has been sitting on this land since the Woodards settled with her. Bonnie had a long-standing argument with Yaley since the lawsuit, but it was not enough to kill her. Plus, Bonnie had an alibi with a client. She was showing property at the time of Yaley's disappearance and death." Hank had already gotten all the pieces together, and they fit perfectly in my head as he told us how the entire situation leading up to today had played out.

"Ted told her Yaley had told him about an argument between her and Shane. Yaley said Shane was mad she wouldn't put the distillery on the tours for this season, but Yaley couldn't because his paperwork hadn't been filed. It was then that Yaley had figured out that Shane had paid off a couple of board members of the Daniel Boone National Forest to push through his permit."

"That's illegal." Gert's jaw dropped. "We both know what a stickler the board is when it comes to anything to do with the national forests, parks, and the law."

There were so many hoops to jump through and steps to follow. The board didn't make it easy for me to redo the campground when I moved here, and forget about putting a pool in for my guests. Anything that disturbs the natural landscape in a national park was off-limits unless the right environmental engineers, architects, and experts were brought in to give their two cents. That was a long process that could take years.

"It is illegal, and Bonnie knew it. She knew he had gone to the two board members, and she told us about it. We turned it over to the rangers to deal with them legally. But as for Bonnie, she and Yaley were enemies, but that didn't make her the killer." Hank was right.

"There are so many twists to this." I blinked my eyes a few times to try to wrap my head around the motive. "I guess Shane killed Bonnie to keep her quiet. But how did he track down Yaley?"

"From what I understand, Shane had been at the Normal Diner a few days in a row to help Ty Randal with some bourbon-infused recipes. Shane met Joel, and after Joel had left the diner, Ty told him all about Yaley between the time Joel had dropped Yaley off at her home that morning and before she came to the amphitheater. Ty also told Shane about everyone around here and what they do." Hank leaned his elbows on the windowsill.

"Which is the same thing he did for me when I moved here." I clearly remember how everyone knew everything about everyone. Ty and I were very close when I moved here, dated even, and he told me what everyone did for a living, who they were related to, and what they drove.

"Right. So Shane had stored up all the information, and I'd say he kept an eye on Joel and Yaley." Hank gave the windowsill a few quick taps and pushed back up to stand. "We have built a case where we believe he stalked Yaley because he knew she would be a thorn in his side since she knew about the bribing. She'd never let him have any advertising. The only way to get rid of her was to use Joel. We also traced the flowers sent to Yaley back to Shane. He admitted he sent them to try to get her to see his side of things. He also admits he put on there to meet him at the amphitheater but swears he didn't pick her up. He claims he never saw her and left."

"So he was downtown when she disappeared?" My jaw dropped.

"Yes. He said he sent her the flowers. The card had it on there to meet him at the amphitheater. He didn't sign it in hopes she'd think it was Joel and that she'd show up. Which we all know she did." Hank let out a long, deep sigh. "Now we just need a confession from him."

"What about Joel's truck? How did he do that?" I questioned.

"We don't have that information, but we're hoping to get it from him and his fingerprint at the department. Which means I've got to go. It's going to be a long night, so I'm not going to be able to have supper." He put his head back in the window to kiss me.

"Okay." I kissed him, a little embarrassed with Gert right there. "Call me, and let me know what happened."

"I will." He looked over at Gert and waved. "I'll let you know if I need you to come down to give another statement."

"Sure." She nodded. "No problem. I'll talk to you later," she said to me before she got out of the car and went back to her own car.

Hank walked off, and I couldn't help but take one big breath of relief knowing the killer was finally behind bars and that I could go back to the campground so I could call all the guests who had canceled. Surely, they'd come tomorrow, knowing the killer was caught.

There were still so many unanswered questions I had for Hank about Shane and his killing spree. My head continued to wonder how Shane got the truck. And what about Yaley's car? How did it crash? Who crashed it?

It was hard for me to wrap my head around all the things Hank had told me and Gert. I was just going to have to believe he knew what he was doing and how the evidence fit together. Hank was big on evidence and exactly how it all fit together while I was big on common sense.

I'd thought about it so much that I didn't even remember getting from the distillery to the campground. It was as if I blinked, and then I was pulling up the drive of Happy Trails.

"What on earth?" I noticed the lights were on in the office. Dottie never worked past five, and it was just a little past the hour.

Instead of driving on to the RV to let Fifi and Chester out, I decided to run into the office to see what Dottie was doing and to tell her the good news about Shane so we could start calling the canceled reservations back.

"Dottie, why are you still in here?" I opened the door. "Dottie!" I screamed when I saw her lying on the floor, belly down and smoke rolling out of her mouth like a chimney.

I ran over to her but didn't move her. I could see there was something wrong by the way her legs were lying.

"Honey, call 9-1-1. I think I broke a hip." The cigarette bobbed up and down in the corner of her mouth. "I've been lying here waitin' for someone to come in, so I had to smoke to take my mind off the pain. Thank the Lord, my cigarette case was in my pocket."

"Don't move," I instructed her. Since I owned a campground in a national park, it was required by law that I take first aid training, so I knew that moving her could hurt her worse. "Agnes, Dottie has fallen, and we need an ambulance. I think she's broke her hip." I was so happy Agnes Swift had answered the dispatch. "Thank you," I told her after she told me she'd get right on it.

"Are they on their way?" Dottie groaned.

"They are. You just hold tight." I sat down next to her so she wouldn't try to look at me. "How on earth did you fall and land on your belly?"

"You ain't gonna like it." Her face contorted as she winced. "But I passed out again. Low blood sugar."

"Mmm-hhhhh." I bit my tongue so I wouldn't start an argument with her. "I can hear the sirens. They will be right here. I'll be right back."

I got up and left her there to flag down the ambulance just in case they passed the office.

"In here." I pointed to the office and bounced on my toes. "She's broken something. She passed out."

"Low blood sugar." She grimaced when the EMT started to feel around.

"Do you have diabetes?" the EMT asked.

"Nope. Diet," Dottie told them, but they focused on me. I nodded my head.

"Ma'am, your granddaughter says it's diabetes." The EMT looked up at me again.

"Granddaughter?" Dottie jerked then winced in pain. "Ohhh. Ohhh."

"Just stay right there. We'll get you on the board to stabilize your neck and back in case your injury has extended to those areas, but I believe you have a broken bone either in your hip or leg."

"She is my boss." Dottie looked up at me when they flipped her over. "Nosy friend too."

"She has been passing out lately. We went to the ER the other day, and they ran a battery of tests before they discharged her."

"Is 'Dorthea Swaggert' your name?" The EMT was looking at the phone in her hand. "I'm on the hospital portal." She waved it in the air. "Technology." She shrugged. "Anyways…" She rattled off Dottie's personal information so she could let the hospital know they were bringing her in. "It says here that you signed yourself out the other night in the middle of the night."

"You what?" My jaw dropped at the news. "You told me they discharged you. No wonder there weren't any phone calls to me from the hospital staff." I gave her the stink eye with a long sigh, letting go of the fact that she lied to me. "I'll follow behind in my car."

"No. No," Dottie protested. They had already put her on the spinal board with a neck brace to stabilize her. "You go take care of Fifi, and I'll call you."

"Absolutely not." I followed them to the ambulance and confirmed I'd be right there.

Before they could even shut the door, Betts's cleaning van was zooming up the drive, gravel spitting up under the tires.

"What's going on?" Abby jumped out of the van before Betts had applied the brakes. "Betts said she heard on the scanner that Agnes called an ambulance."

"I found her on the floor of the office. She said she passed out, and I think she broke her hip. I'm going to the hospital." I jiggled my keys.

"No! We are going." Betts had rolled down the window. "Jump in!"

It took me a split second to make the decision to leap into the van and go with Abby and Betts to the hospital to support Dottie. While Betts followed closely behind the ambulance, I quickly texted Hank to let him know what I was doing and called Henry to see if he wouldn't mind letting the dogs out.

Of course Henry was more than willing and sounded very concerned about Dottie. I told him she was still her ornery self, and I'd keep him posted.

"Could life get any crazier right now?" I asked Betts and Abby. "I mean, all of this seems to be happening all at once. Yaley's murder, Dottie passing out, Joel being a suspect, and now Bonnie Turner dead with Shane Holland as the killer the entire time."

"Wait?" Abby jerked around. "What? Shane Holland? Bonnie Turner is dead?"

"You two better hold on, I'm about to take you on a wild ride." I told them about Bonnie threatening me when I was at the undercroft of the Normal Baptist Church.

"I wondered why you left so quickly." Betts pulled into the emergency room parking lot while I kept my eye on the ambulance as they backed up to the emergency patient entrance.

"I don't think Bonnie had a clue what I knew, but I do think she thought I knew how they'd practically stolen the land from Yaley and Ted." We got out of the van, and from a distance, we waved at Dottie when the emergency room staff whisked her away.

While we waited in the waiting room for someone to come tell us about the results from the X-rays they'd taken from Dottie, I told them how Gert had to pick up the bourbon barrel lids from Shane and had invited me to go tour the place.

"Abby, you knew I was going to go there. And when you had to cancel our tour, I knew I had to jump at the opportunity to go with Gert." I proceeded to tell them how Shane was showing us around the distillery and how, when he opened the barrel, Bonnie's hand popped out. "That pink scarf she had tied around her neck was in her hand."

"Come on." Abby smiled. "You're saying that Shane Holland killed Bonnie Turner because she was holding the bribe over his head, which is possible. But why would he take you and Gert to the warehouse or wherever you were if he'd killed Bonnie and dumped her body in some bourbon? Come on."

"I don't know all the details. I just know that Hank felt pretty confident they had their man. But the fingerprints they've not been able to identify on Yaley's necklace and her purse will definitely be compared to Shane's." I looked up when I noticed a doctor was walking toward us.

I wanted to talk to Abby and Betts a little more about what Abby had brought up. It was a great point, and as much as I wanted to think Hank had put all the pieces together with the killer in jail, Abby made me second-guess him.

CHAPTER SIXTEEN

I wished the doctor would've had better news about Dottie's broken hip and how she had to go straight into surgery in the morning. They were going to keep her as pain free as possible, and even though she put on a brave face for me, Abby, and Betts, I could see the pain in her eyes.

With her encouragement and the fact the nursing staff was keeping her pretty doped up with some heavy painkillers, making her sleep, I agreed to leave with Betts and Abby but promised I'd be back in the morning.

"What are you going to do tonight? Do we need to keep you company?" Betts offered for her and Abby to hang around the campground with me. "We can get some work around the campground done. Whatever you need."

"It's still early." Abby made a good point about how daylight savings time created longer days. The sun wouldn't even be going down until closer to nine, which made it feel more like four o'clock than eight.

"No. I'm going to actually just forget about calling the reservations who canceled. It just seems like one thing after the other is telling me to let it go." I wasn't big into superstition, but there was no denying the fact that every time I thought I was going to be able to make good with the canceled guests, something else popped up, making it virtually impossible to continue with opening the season this week. "I think I'm going to take Fifi and Chester for their walk, maybe grill a hot dog on a campfire, and go to bed."

"I'll pick you up to take you to the hospital." Betts and I had decided to come for Dottie's surgery because Abby and Queenie both had to work. Queenie had moved her earlier Jazzercise classes to tonight because the repast cooking had taken place during her class.

"Are you sure we can't stay to keep you company?" Abby questioned. "I know I would love to take the dogs for a walk. Betts can go home, and you can take me home later."

"If you want to stay, you can, but you don't have to. I'm always up for company, but I'm really fine." I was blessed to have such great friends who really wanted to make sure I was okay.

"Are you sure?" Abby gave me a sideways glance.

"I promise. I'm exhausted and really need to get some sleep before tomorrow, so I'm sure my walk with the dogs will be a quick one." I felt my body relax as we pulled into the campground. "Just let me off at the office. I parked my car there."

When we pulled up, Henry had Chester and Fifi on the dock while he used the pond rake to grab any extra moss that had formed. Fifi's ears perked up when she heard the van park.

"I'll see you tomorrow," I told Betts. "Abby, have a good day at work. I'll be fine," I assured them when I noticed they'd given each other the look where they were trying to decide if they should stay with me.

"Thanks, Henry!" I yelled over after Fifi and Chester darted toward me. I bent down to let them rub and jump on me while I gave them a few good pats. "Let's go check the messages."

The three of us headed inside the office. I hit the Play button and cleaned up all the papers that'd fallen on the floor when Dottie had taken her spill. There was a message from one of the honeymooners who had initially canceled, along with three more families who had canceled. They'd heard Normal was safe and sound, so they were still coming, putting me in overdrive to really make sure all of their accommodations were ready before they got here tomorrow at noon.

Even Joel Grassle had called.

"Hey, Mae, it's Joel. I took your advice and started to write down things I've remembered that Yaley had mumbled when she broke up with me. She honestly made no sense but talked about new trails and how she wasn't going to be able to do her job and something about moving away. If I remember anything else, I'll let you know. I would've called your cell, but I don't have the number, and Bobby Ray has left for the night."

"New trails?" I questioned and flipped Fifi and Chester a treat. "There's always new trails popping up." I talked to the fur babies as if they understood everything I was saying. "Unfortunately, those new trails are blazed from people who go off-trail hiking when they shouldn't."

It was one of the dangerous facts we tried to tell hikers and campers who were new to the Daniel Boone National Forest. Every time I saw campers from my campground heading out to hike, I'd tell them to make sure they stay on the paths that are marked with the national park symbol. Those were the real trails, and any offshoots were not made or maintained by the park, which could become very dangerous with drop-offs and even wildlife.

When the rangers were called about missing hikers, nine times out of ten, the hiker was safely found on a trail that wasn't a real trail.

"People need to follow the rules." I grabbed the extra leashes I had in the office and flung them over my shoulder. "Who wants to go for a nice walk?"

Fifi and Chester danced around my feet. They darted out the door before I could get the thing fully open and straight across the parking lot, past Dottie's camper, and into the woods.

"Where are y'all going?" I questioned and headed down the marked trail right behind Dottie's camper.

It was one of the moderate trails that Fifi and I were used to, but I was not sure how familiar Chester was with it. He and Hank did do some hiking without me and Fifi, but I never really asked what trails they took.

Chester seemed to know. He darted off down the path, and before I could keep up with him, I heard him barking like the hunting dog he used to be.

Fifi wasn't as brave as Chester. She hung back with me.

"Chester! Come here!" I demanded of the dog, though I was happy he was still barking so we could find him. Even though Hank had gotten him after an investigation, he'd grown to love the pup, and I couldn't even imagine if I lost him or worse…let some sort of wildlife kill him.

"The Daniel Boone National Forest had the trail on the registry," I told Fifi and pushed away any of the branches dangling down into the path.

I knew every trail around Happy Trails or near Happy Trails, so this was probably one of those trails that were forged by a group of yearly hikers who enjoyed spending weekends in the forest without adhering to the rules. Hank used to tell me stories about how he'd spent most of his time tracking down the people who made these trails, and here we were, hiking on down it.

Chester's bark was getting louder and louder with each step I took, so I knew we were close to him. The deeper into the woods I followed the homemade trail, the more intrigued I became to see where it led and exactly what Chester had found.

When I came to the clearing, I was a little taken aback by the five or six tents that were set up. Chester was going from tent to tent, barking and growling.

"Tourists," I groaned and recalled what Hank thought about them.

"Those were the types of tourists we didn't want in Normal." I could hear Hank now. He believed it was due to these types of campers who dropped tents, smoked pot, drank, and left their trash for us locals to deal with. In fact, the few fires we'd had in the Daniel Boone National Forest were started by these visitors who had no regard about camping or keeping our park clean or safe.

"Chester!" I hollered from the edge of the clearing and bent down to clip the leash on Fifi's collar.

"Hey buddy." I heard a familiar voice as someone emerged from a tent.

"Skip," I greeted Skip Toliver as relief settled over me. "I'm so glad it's you. I was afraid Chester used his crazy hunting skills to find some sort of pot field or something Hank is always trying to find."

Skip and I started to walk toward each other. Chester darted off behind the tents into the wooded area.

"Chester!" I screamed.

"What if Yaley had stuck her nose into something that it wasn't supposed to be stuck in? She got caught up in it and decided she was going to take matters into her own hands by threatening to go to the authorities." Skip spread his arms open. "You were almost right." He pushed up the bandana he had holding back his curly hair.

"Right?" A nervous laugh escaped me. Chester's bark had abruptly stopped. "Chester!" I called and looked past Skip.

"When I talked to you downtown outside of that hair place..." He snapped his fingers and looked up as if he was searching for the name.

"Cute-icles?" I questioned and wondered if what my gut was saying about Skip Toliver was true. "Chester!" I nervously screamed in hopes to get him and get out of there.

Was he Yaley's killer? Was he Bonnie's killer?

"What are you saying, Skip?" I had to know. "Good boy!" I yelled when I saw Chester come back with a stick in his mouth. I was so grateful to be getting out of there.

"You are a good boy." Skip bent down and plucked the leafy vine out of Chester's mouth. "But these are new babies, and you shouldn't have picked this one."

The last little bit of daylight was about to go down past the trees, but I could clearly see the leafy plant Skip was twirling in his finger and thumb.

"You see, Yaley was hiking some new trails, and she just so happened upon my little secret." He was clearly telling me without telling me he was growing pot in the forest. "She said that I had to come clean to the authorities, or she wouldn't put my whitewater rafting and canoe business in her tour schedule." He carefully untied the bandana and pulled it taut.

"I'm guessing you're getting good at strangling women." I gulped and felt my neck tighten. "How did you do it? How did you pull it off?"

"Easy. When you're as low-key as I am, no one around here notices you. I don't make money on the whitewater gig, but I make a ton off the pot, and I'm not willing to give it up. I know these trails like the back of my hand. I know where they lead and where they end." He talked and twisted the bandana as though he was mentally sizing up my neck and how much strength it was going to take to get it around my neck.

I dropped Fifi's leash in hopes she'd run back to the campground, but she didn't. Faithful Fifi stood right there with me, Chester, and Skip.

"I heard Yaley and Joel break up one night right outside of the tree line near his backyard. I kept an eye on her in case she told anyone about the pot. She didn't, but she threatened me. I also overheard Joel on the phone with Steve about picking up his car." He had such a pleased look on his face.

"How did you pick her up? How did you know?" I couldn't imagine.

"What part of me keeping an eye on her every day are you not getting?" He spoke to me as if I was stupid, and I didn't like that at all. "I know every single trail from here to the Sierra Club offices. I watched the delivery people deliver the flowers. I heard her read the envelope from the open window. It was perfect. It was like it was meant to be. I heard her call Joel and leave him a message about meeting him. I ran through the forest and slipped out of the woods to where the junkyard is located. I took the truck."

"And she just got into the truck with you?" I couldn't imagine if Yaley had something over him that she'd trust him like that.

"Oh no. She was definitely hesitant. The power of love is strong." The corner of his lip twitched up. "I told her I was at the gas station, and Joel had an accident. He had me take his truck to meet up with her.

I merely suggested she get in, and I'd take her to him. That's when it was easy. I always heard Joel's truck rumble through Happy Trails, so I simply dumped her body in your dumpster. I never figured you'd find her. Which is unfortunate for you."

I put my hand out to stop him from walking toward me. Chester moved in between us. Skip looked down at him and stopped.

"What about Bonnie?" I had to know how he pulled that one off.

"She was a little trickier. After Yaley went missing, she showed up at the river and asked me if I had anything to do with Yaley going missing. She said she knew Yaley had something over me, and Yaley was going to tell them why she refused to put my gig on the tour schedule at the meeting that afternoon. I played dumb but knew I had to get rid of her." He gripped the bandana with both hands. "She was a little harder to follow, but there was one place she always showed up. That new bourbon place. I had to jump on it when she showed up there today. I stuck her body in an open bourbon barrel and skedaddled."

"I-I…" I stammered when I saw I wasn't going to get out of there without a fight.

"I really liked you too. But you date Hank, and Hank hates people like me." He shrugged as if he had no other option before he leapt forward, using his foot to trip me to the ground.

Before I knew what was happening, my head bounced on the ground, and he slipped the bandana around my neck and threw me over on my stomach, my hands up under me and his knee in my back. He twisted and twisted the cloth until I was gasping for breath.

"Pha…pha…" I wanted to beg for my life. I tried to kick him with the heels of my shoes, but his body was up on my back so far that I couldn't reach him.

The sounds around me became silent. I gave one last thrust of my legs before, out of the corner of my eye, I saw Chester jump in the air with his mouth wide-open. He clamped down on Skip Toliver's arm.

"I'll kill you." Skip fell off me. His arm was covered in blood. He tried to grab Chester a few times when Chester got between me and him.

Chester moved into a downward-dog position with his butt in the air, his teeth gnawing against each other. I scrambled to my heinie and gasped for air as I scooted back to sitting.

"No one, not even your little dogs, will get out of here alive." Skip used the bandana as a tourniquet, wrapping it around the dog bite.

A gunshot rang out like a firework. I threw my hands over my head to protect myself.

"Hold it right there!" someone yelled from the edge of the woods. "I swear I'll shoot you."

Bert Erickson, in his tiny running shorts and tank top, moved into the clearing with the gun set on Skip. With the gun on Skip and Chester still growling, I felt safe standing up.

"Call your boyfriend." Bert threw me his cell phone.

"Thanks, mine is in my purse at the campground." My hands shook while I tried to recall and dial Hank's number from memory.

"I never jog without my cell or my gun because you never know what kind of crazies you might run into out here." Bert walked closer to Skip, keeping the gun pointed on him the entire time.

CHAPTER SEVENTEEN

"Lookee at that," Dottie snarled from the bed. The lower half of her body was in a cast from the hip break. She pointed out the door of her room at the older man rolling down the hall in a wheelchair. "This place is for old people. I want to go home."

Betts, Abby, Queenie, and I planted smiles on our faces so we wouldn't give into Dottie's negative attitude she'd had since the doctor ordered her to make a full recovery in the live-in rehabilitation center. That news didn't sit well with Dottie, giving me a headache, and it'd only been a week since her surgery.

The care facility was very nice. Dottie had her own room with a bathroom and a spectacular view of a pond. There was a bridge leading out to a gazebo in the middle of the pond. Today, there were a few people out there reading.

"Don't you worry about anyone in here but yourself." Queenie hopped up out of the chair and grapevined over to the door to shut it. "If you do what the doctor says, then you might get out of here faster. I can give you a few strength exercises."

Dottie snarled then fixed her attention upon me.

"So tell me all about where the case is now." She was talking about

Yaley Woodard's murder and all the secrets that'd gotten swept right on out from underneath the rug.

"I read that Ted Woodard wasn't going to press any sort of extortion charges," Abby commented. She was leaning up against the ledge of the big window that overlooked the pond. The sun was shining and cast a shadow of Abby on the floor of Dottie's room.

"Technically, he can't anyways. Though it was extortion, wasn't it?" Betts confused us all. "Ted and Yaley willingly gave the property over to Bonnie without question. She didn't forcibly make them give her the land. In the eyes of the court, they offered her the land in exchange for the money Ted and Yaley had put her out in rent when Yaley was really illegally funneling all the tourist accommodations to her brother's property." She sighed. "Both parties were doing illegal things, so it kinda evens them out in Ted's eyes."

"That's so crazy. It makes my head spin." Dottie laid her head back on her flat pillow.

I walked over and fluffed it up so she could try to rest better. She looked up at me. Her eyes softened, and we smiled at each other.

"I just can't get over Skip Toliver growing illegal pot and right behind my house." Dottie huffed. "I sure could use a cigarette."

"Now is the time to quit that," Queenie snapped at Dottie.

"I was so shocked about it, too, but Agnes Swift did mention that Jerry had been really cracking down on the illegal growers." I took the conversation back from Queenie. The last thing Dottie needed was to be fussed at. Her fuse was already so short that she was about to explode.

"I'm glad Bert Erickson came along the way he did." Abby's eyes grew. "And to think he jogs with a gun. That's some talent. I'd be afraid to shoot my foot off."

We all laughed. Even Dottie.

"There's the real hero," I said, my eyes lighting up when Hank walked into Dottie's room with Chester on a leash.

"Nah." Hank waved off my comment.

"I wasn't talking about you." I bent down, and Chester ran over to me. "I'm talking about you," I baby-talked Chester. "If it weren't for your furious growl and bite, I might have been strangled."

"Hunting dog turned police canine." Hank walked over to Dottie's bed. "How are you doing? Need anything?"

"Nah. I'm fine." Dottie patted his hand. "I just can't get over it."

"Yeah. Yaley's final autopsy report came back, and she was strangled like Bonnie. We even found Yaley's heart pendant from her necklace in one of the tents. I hate it too. Skip could've had a great business with the whitewater rafting and canoes if he'd just stuck with it." Hank shook his head.

"What is going to happen with the distillery and the board members who were bribed by Shane Holland?" Betts asked.

"The distillery will be fine. Shane had to pay a hefty fine, and the board members resigned, though we couldn't find the money trail where Shane had bribed them. The only thing we could fine him on was the dates on the permit were too soon." He walked over and put his arm around me. "Didn't Mae tell you the news?"

"What news?" Queenie asked. All of them looked at me.

"They asked me to take one of the vacant positions on the board." I wasn't sure what I was going to do. I didn't know all the rules and regulations regarding the Daniel Boone National Forest to even feel qualified.

"You're going to do it, right?" Abby asked with excitement.

"I'm thinking about it. With Dottie gone for a few weeks, I've got a lot to do at the campground." I looked over at Dottie. She was awfully quiet for Dottie. "You okay?"

"I'm fine. I just want out of here," she spat with a curled nose. "And Hank," Dottie called, waving him back over.

"Yes, ma'am." He walked back to her bed.

"You just make sure all the things are getting done around the campground while I'm gone." She wagged her finger at him. "Don't you let her replace me either."

"Dottie, do you think anyone can replace you?" I asked her, standing up.

"Never." Dottie's mouth grew into a big grin.

All of us belted out in laughter. Even Chester barked. That's when I knew that everything was going to be okay. Dottie would do her rehab and be back in no time. All was going to be good in the camper-hood.

THE END

If you enjoyed reading this book as much as I enjoyed writing it then be sure to return to the Amazon page and leave a review.

Go to Tonyakappes.com for a full reading order of my novels and while there join my newsletter. You can also find links to Facebook, Instagram and Goodreads.

Want more of Mae West and the Laundry Club Ladies?

Be sure you turn the page to read a sneak peek of Kickbacks, Kayaks, & Kidnapping. Or you can purchase a copy of Kickbacks, Kayaks, & Kidnapping at Amazon or read for FREE in Kindle Unlimited.

BUT WAIT! Readers ask me how much my cozy mysteries and the characters in them reflect my real life. Well...here is a good story for you.

Whooo hooo!! I'm so glad we are a week out from last Coffee Chat with Tonya and happy to report the poison ivy is almost gone! But y'all we got more issues than Time magazine up in our family.

When y'all ask me if my real life ever creeps into books, well...grab your coffee because here is a prime example!

My sweet mom's birthday was over the weekend. Now, I'd already decided me and Rowena was going to stay there for a couple of extra days.

On her birthday, Sunday, Tracy and David were there too, and we were talking about what else...poison ivy! I was telling them how I can't stand not shaving my legs. Mom and Tracy told me they don't shave daily and I might've curled my nose a smidgen. And apparently it didn't go unnoticed.

I went inside the house to start cooking breakfast for everyone and mom went up to her room to get her bathing suit on and Tracy was with me. All the men were already outside on the porch.

The awfulest crash came from upstairs and my sister tore out of that kitchen like a bat out of hell and I kept flipping the bacon. My mom had fallen...shaving her legs!

Great. Now it's my fault.

Her wrist was a little stiff but she kept saying she was fine. We had a great day. We celebrated her birthday, swam, and had cake. When it came time for everyone to leave but me and Ro, I told mom that she should probably go get an x-ray because her wrist was a little swollen.

After a lot of coaxing, she agreed and I put my shoes on and told Tracy, David, and Eddy to go on home and we'd call them.

My mama looked me square in the face and said, "You're going with that top knot on your head?"

I said, "yes."

She sat back down in the chair and said, "I'm not going with you lookin' like that."

"Are you serious?" I asked.

"Yes. I'm dead serious. I'm not going with you looking like that. What if we see someone?" She was serious, y'all!

She protested against my hair!

Now...this is exactly like the southern mama's I write about! I looked at Eddy and he was laughing. Tracy and David were laughing and I said, "I can't wait until I tell my coffee chat people about this."

As you can see in the above photo, the before and after photo.

Yep...we went and she broke her wrist! Can you believe that? We were a tad bit shocked, and I'll probably be staying a few extra days (which will give us even more to talk about over coffee next week).

Oh...we didn't see anyone we knew so I could've worn my top knot! As I'm writing this, you can bet your bottom dollar my hair is pulled up in my top knot!

Okay, so y'all might be asking why I'm putting this little story in the back of my book, well, that's a darn tootin' good question.

This is exactly what you can expect when you sign up for my newsletter. There's always something going on in my life that I have to chat with y'all about each Tuesday on Coffee Chat with Tonya. Go to Tonyakappes.com and click on subscribe in the upper right corner to join.

Chapter One of Book Twelve
Kickbacks, Kayaks, & Kidnapping

Entrepreneur.

I mentally read the word I'd written on a piece of paper in the notebook the Laundry Club gals and I kept handy for when we'd put on our amateur sleuth hats. We'd use it to write down clues that helped us put two and two together.

"Entrepreneur." I read the word out loud, smiling a little. I tucked a strand of my long curly brown hair behind my ear as I let out a long sigh.

Fifi, my toy poodle, jumped up on the small couch in our RV and wedged her head up under my arm.

"How do you think 'Mae West, entrepreneur' sounds?" I asked her.

She jumped up and swiped her tongue along my cheek.

"I knew you'd love it." I sighed and picked up the copy of National Park Magazine I'd been reading a few minutes earlier when I saw the ad Abby Fawn, a good friend of mine and librarian at Normal Library, had placed as my social media guru for Happy Trails Campground.

The ad was for the new water activities I'd added to the campground activities: kayaking, canoeing, white-water rafting, and fishing. Until recently, I had been able to let my guests know about a company that provided these activities, but that company folded. It left me the opportunity to literally dip my toe into the water of extra outdoor activities, which led to more money on the bottom dollar for the campground.

Since the company had folded due to the owner going to prison, the price was pretty cheap. One problem: I knew nothing about kayaking or canoeing, much less white-water rafting. That's when I decided it would be fun to host a weeklong summer festival called Paddle Fest.

Since Abby knew all things about the Daniel Boone National Forest, where Normal, Kentucky and Happy Trails Campground were located, she'd told me about how years ago, the forest hosted an actual kayak competition. Who knew there was such a thing?

In fact, there was even a kayaking team at the local high school. It would be perfect for kick-starting my new adventure. . .which made me, Maybelline Grant West, an entrepreneur.

"Right here." I pointed at the ad to show Fifi. "It's in fine print at the bottom, but it says Mae West, entrepreneur." I squinted to look at the fine print Abby had put in the ad.

Fifi seemed to like it. Her stubby tail wagged so fast. She did a few twirls that completely warranted praise.

After all, she had been a pedigreed show poodle until she crossed to the wrong side of the campground where Ethel kept Rosco, her male bulldog, off leash. Most dogs weren't on leashes in the campground—at the owners' own risk since we did have some coyotes and some brown bears—so I, too, was at fault for letting Fifi run around when I had only been babysitting her. It was only at night that I would put her on a leash.

To say it nicely, Fifi had gotten pregnant, and it was her ticket to freedom from performing all those tricks. Plus, her owner had only used Fifi for the pedigree and saw to it that I take responsibility for the chaos I'd caused by taking Fifi off her hands—life changing for me and Fifi. Keeping her had been the best decision I'd ever made. Well, that and the decision I'd made not to sell the campground, making Normal my new home and living in an RV.

Talk about life changing. All my adult life, I'd lived in New York City after I escaped the foster care system in Kentucky. It wasn't until I met and married one of the wealthiest, and oldest, businessmen in the stock market—who just so happened to go to federal prison, causing me to lose my Manhattan apartment and our Hamptons home—did I find out I was the owner of Happy Trails Campground. I'd spent the last few years bringing it and the tourism of Normal back to life, making me the entrepreneur.

"I think. . ." The creak of the metal camper step up to my door told me someone was about to knock before their fist made contact with the metal around the screen door.

"Mae, you in there?" Dottie Swaggert's face was barely visible through the screen, but her hot-pink hair curlers practically glowed in the darkness of the night. It was her deep Southern drawl that told me it was her.

"Come on in." I slid the magazine over the notebook just as she swung open the door. Fifi jumped off the couch and happily greeted one of her favorite people.

"What are you doing up so late?" Her eyes zeroed in on the small dinette table. She put her hand down to pat Fifi. "Are you moonlighting on the gals?"

She moved her hand from Fifi to one of the curlers that'd come unsnapped around a piece of her thick red hair. Within a second, she'd rolled the hair right back around the sponge and made sure it was snapped close to her head.

"Moonlighting? Are you kidding? I'm already exhausted from running this place." I showed her the magazine. "Abby's ad came out for the locals to enter the kayak competition this week, and I can't wait."

"The ad she ran a couple of months ago pretty much filled it up. Do you know we have people coming from all over the country to compete?" She shook her head and made herself comfortable on the couch.

Fifi took it as an opportunity to score more loving by lying next to Dottie.

I'd never even known camping was so popular or everything that went with it. When I'd first shown up in Normal to check out this new owner-ship of mine, the place was so run-down, it took every bit of anything I could pawn, sell, and barter to get it cleaned up enough to open.

Not to mention what it took to make the RV my home. When I looked around, I was pretty proud of all the elbow grease I'd put into the place.

I'd used every bit of space possible. I took down all the walls to create an open-concept plan with the kitchen and family room in one big room. I put up shiplap walls and painted them white. I'd gotten a cute café table with two chairs and a small leather couch from the Tough Nickel, the local thrift store. I'd even redone all the floors with luxurious vinyl that resembled grey wood flooring. The kitchen cabinets and all the storage cabinets were white. I'd transformed my little camper into a charming country farmhouse décor.

I'd strung twinkle lights everywhere I could. The bathroom had been updated with a tile shower and upgraded toilet, which was nice. My bedroom was located in the back. I'd opted to buy a new mattress, with some wooden pallets painted pink and nailed together as a headboard. I'd gotten a dresser from the Tough Nickel that went perfectly with my distressed look. The fuzzy rugs and milk glass vases that were currently filled with different floral arrangements from the Sweet Smell Flower Shop, the local florist, were the perfect romantic touch, especially now since I'd been dating Hank Sharp.

"I'm not sure why you keep spending money to put ads in all them papers and magazines since we ain't got no place to put people." Dottie snarled. "We've been booked for months."

"Thanks to a great manager like you." I knew a little praise went a long way with her. "Just because we are booked doesn't mean other people from the other campgrounds can't participate. They will see how awesome our campground is and want to go ahead and book for next year."

It was crazy how the campground was booked up for months. Cancellations went out every Tuesday morning at eight a.m., and we'd book back up within a few minutes of the emails going out.

"I guess I'm not complaining. It's good to have a steady job." Dottie had recently had a bout of fainting issues that resulted in her falling down and breaking a hip.

She'd lived in a local rehab facility while she got back up on her feet, which made her none too happy. The Laundry Club gals, our small group of friends, and I took turns visiting her day in and day out so Dottie didn't have to be alone.

The Laundry Club gals were a big reason I'd decided to stay in Normal and make it my home. The Laundry Club was the name of the laundromat in Normal, where I had to do laundry when I first moved there since the laundry room at the campground wasn't working. There, I'd met the owner, Betts Hager, along with Queenie French and Abby Fawn. They were all friends with Dottie, and it just so happened to be the place where all four of them hung out.

Years later, we all still met there for book club, coffee, and social hour. Plus, there was a police scanner there. Talk about hours of entertainment. The National Park Rangers along with the police department got several crazy calls every night. Campers got themselves into some crazy situations. We loved meeting up at the Laundry Club and gathering around the scanner to see what was going to happen next. Sometimes we'd jump into Betts's old cleaning van and go see what all the commotion was about. Especially when there was a death.

It seemed a little morbid, but we did it anyway. That's where the notebook came in handy. There'd been a few murders in these parts. Since it was a national forest and park, people figured they could just hide a body out here and it would never be found.

Somehow, one of the Laundry Club ladies or I would always discover or happen upon some sort of murder that put us in the thick of things, which was when we'd put clues in the notebook so we'd have them all in one place.

"I've been writing down ideas for the festival for next year in the notebook since we've not used it in a while." I set the magazine back down on the small café table and took a good look at Dottie. "Are you out doing your physical therapy?"

She grimaced when she moved, but she tried to hide it from me.

"I'm trying, but I still can't get good sleep with this new hip," she moaned and rubbed her side.

"You're just a couple of months out." I slipped on my flip-flops. "Come on. I'll go a time or two around with you."

I walked over to the couch and helped her up. It wasn't too late. I figured it to be around ten or so, since right before she'd gotten here, the night had turned completely dark. During the summer, it was still light out until nine thirty, which made the campground stay alive until around midnight.

The smell of the campfires was carried on the light breeze as it came through the open windows of the RV. It was a good time to walk around the campground and say hello to our guests.

I made sure we knew all of them by name when they arrived.

"I don't need to bother you with walking me around like an old lady," she grumbled and got to her feet.

"You are an old lady," I teased, and she smacked me away. "We need to say goodnight to our guests. Remember, that's why we are in for the Campground Hospitality Award."

It was an honor to be in the running for the award with so many campgrounds in and around the national park. When I'd gotten word that we were up for it along with five other campgrounds, I knew we had it in the bag.

At least that's what I told myself, determined to win. There was a competitive streak in me that I'd never been able to tame.

"Oh, they did put up the banner late this evening." Dottie had told me the national park committee had called to let us know they were placing banners at each campground. "They had sent over the ballots for people too."

"We need to make sure to distribute those tomorrow at the hospitality room." I made a mental note to grab those in the morning from the office since it was my shift to open and take them to the recreational room, where there was complimentary coffee from Trails Coffee and donuts from the Cookie Crumble Bakery.

Both businesses were locally owned. I made sure when I opened the campground that I would feature local products and businesses so if the guests liked them, they'd go visit the businesses and purchase. It was a foolproof business plan that'd brought Normal back as a thriving community and got me the key to the city. . .which brought me back to the title "entrepreneur."

I couldn't help but swell up with pride when we stepped out of the

RV and looked out across the lake in the middle of the campground with all the campfires dancing under the dark night sky.

"We sure have come a long way," I told Dottie as we walked around the lake on the far side, near the bungalow section of Happy Trails. "I guess I never figured we'd have all the bungalows filled as well as all the little campers."

"It was all that fixin' up you've been doing. Making them so popular with the young folks, old folks, and families." She pointed to the largest of the bungalows, where we could see right into the large window.

The family who had rented it had planned their family vacation here. They were sitting inside around the large kitchen table playing a board game. During the day, they'd been busy hiking all the trails that started in the campground. Tomorrow, they were going to go explore some of the hidden waterfalls.

"This one is still my favorite camper." I pointed to the small canned-ham red camper that was a single. It was the cutest. It was very popular and always had a waiting list.

"I know." Dottie stopped and pulled out the cigarette case. She snapped it open and batted out one of her stogies.

I'd really hoped she was going to break that habit when she was in the rehab center, but I now thought rehab had made it worse. Every time I'd go see her, she was having herself a big time, sitting outside with other residents, laughing and talking and all of them smoking too.

"How y'all doin'?" Dottie asked a group of campers when we passed by another one of our campers they'd rented.

She meandered over to their fire while I waited for Fifi to catch up to me on her small walk. That's mostly what we did at night when she was on the leash, but since there were so many people up and fires going, I knew it would be safe for her to walk around without worrying about a coyote snatching her up.

There were a few people sitting on the dock that jutted out on the lake. The paddleboats were pulled up in their places, and Henry was locking them up. Henry Bryan was the handyman who had already worked here, just like Dottie, so it was natural to keep them both on staff. They were the only employees I had, and they were worth their weight in gold.

"Mae, this here is the state kayak champ who is going to be trying out for the next Olympic team." Dottie's accent got stronger as the excitement grew in her voice.

By the way the group of young people laughed, I could tell Dottie entertained them.

"Welcome to Happy Trails." I wanted to make sure we gave a proper hello to our future Olympian. "Are you going to be participating in the kayak race?"

"Of course he is." A young woman got up from the campfire and took her place next to him. "I'm Alli Shelton, Bryce Anderson's agent."

She had long straight brown hair, with all the pieces around her face pulled back into a clip that fastened at the back of her head. The big black-rimmed glasses took up a lot of her forehead and cheeks. From what I could see, she didn't have on any makeup other than maybe a hint of lip balm—not exactly what I assumed for an agent.

Not that people got all dolled up when they went camping, but in her case, renting one of my fanciest campers, I'd say she was glamping it.

"Nice to meet you." Hmm. . .I gave her a once-over as best I could, given it was dark out. By the way she held herself, I could tell she was also an entrepreneur, being an agent and all. "Bryce, we are honored to have you here."

I made another mental note to be sure to look up kayaking, the Olympics, and Bryce when I made it into town tomorrow.

"You are the owner of the campground?" Alli asked me. I nodded. "And you're the one putting on the kayak race, correct?"

"I am. If there's anything you need, please just ask." There was no doubt in my mind she would take me up on my offer.

"Oh, don't worry. Bryce gets whatever it is he wants." She glanced his way, but he'd already gone back to the campfire, where he was doing a couple of shots with a few of the others. "If you'll excuse me, I need to go talk to him, but I do want to come visit you in the morning to discuss his training while we are here and what times we'd like you to shut down the water activities."

"Shut down?" I questioned and looked at Dottie after Alli rushed off. "Does she expect me to shut down the waterway for him to practice?"

"I guess she thinks his you-know-what don't stink and he gets what he wants." Dottie's lit cigarette bounced from the corner of her mouth as she talked.

Both of us stood there and watched as Bryce and Alli had a disagreement. Apparently, from what I'd overheard, she wasn't happy with him drinking and thought he needed to get some sleep. After he told her to lighten up, she stormed off in the direction of one of the little red campers she'd rented while he casually made his way over to another set of campers filled with some college girls taking a summer girls' trip, not caring one bit about the Paddle Fest.

"He don't give one iota about kayaking." Dottie nudged me when Bryce grabbed a girl by the hand. "That woman is right. That boy gets whatever it is he wants."

They disappeared down the mouth of the closest trail.

"Mm-hmm," I said, smiling, "and he's gonna get some chiggers in places he don't want too."

Kickbacks, Kayaks, & Kidnapping is now available to purchase or in Kindle Unlimited.

RECIPES AND CLEANING HACKS FROM MAE WEST AND THE LAUNDRY CLUB LADIES AT THE HAPPY TRAILS CAMPGROUND IN NORMAL KENTUCKY.

SKILLET BACON CINNAMON ROLLS

INGREDIENTS

- A can of Pillsbury Grands! Cinnamon rolls
- 5 slices of cooked bacon
- a 12 inch pre- seasoned skillet

DIRECTIONS

1. First, cook your bacon until it's nicely done with a little bit of soft fat still remaining.

2. Peel apart each cinnamon bun just enough to lay that piece of bacon inside then roll it back up again, pinching the dough to seal it up.

3. Place the buns in a well-seasoned skillet with room between them.

4. Place these over the campfire by covering them in tinfoil to ensure that the heat is kept inside. You will have to watch the bottoms like a hawk.

5. Slather on the icing and enjoy!

Camping Hacks

Know Your Wood – There are two types of wood when it comes to maintaining a campfire, softwood, and hardwood. Softwoods, pines or firs ,will light easier but will burn down quickly. This makes softwoods great for the early stages of a campfire while you're in the building stage. Hardwoods, oak, maple, and ash, will not light as quickly but have long burn times. Making hardwoods great for maintaining a fire without having to constantly add new wood. So be sure to check out what Softwoods and Hardwoods look like. Even take photos of them on your phone so when you're in the wild looking for the best wood for your campfire, you have photos to match up.

Campfire Meatballs

INGREDIENTS

- 1 pound lean ground beef
- 1/4 cup Italian style bread crumbs
- 1 egg, slightly beaten
- 1/2 teaspoon garlic powder
- 1 teaspoon onion powder
- 1 teaspoon dried Italian seasoning
- ½ teaspoon each salt and black pepper
- 1 (24 oz) jar marinara sauce
- Grated Parmesan cheese, as desired, for serving

DIRECTIONS

1. Preheat the grill to medium-high heat or get the campfire started.

2. In a medium-sized bowl, combine the ground beef, breadcrumbs, 1/4 cup marinara sauce, egg, and seasonings; mix well. Shape into meatballs, each about 1 1/4 inches across.

3. Cut pieces of aluminum foil about 18″ x 12″ each. Place equal amounts of the meatballs in the center of each piece of foil. Top each meatball with 3-4 tablespoons marinara sauce. Fold the short ends of the foil together over the center and seal, allowing room for expansion and circulation. Fold in the open edges, sealing each packet securely.

4. Place the packets on the grill for 20 to 25 minutes, or until no pink remains in the meat, turning the packets over once during the grilling.

5. Carefully open the tops of the packets to avoid steam burns and sprinkle with cheese just before serving. Enjoy!

Black Out RV Curtains

If you're like me, you like it to be nice and dark when sleeping. In a RV sometimes you park near bright lights or even parks have overhead lights that shine in through the RV curtains. An easy way to make black out curtains is to simply purchase sticky Velcro from a fabric store to the backside of your curtain at the top. Use Velcro to attach your own black-out lining to your curtain panels! It'll change your life!

CAMPFIRE BREAKFAST HAMBURGER

INGREDIENTS

- 2 cups flour
- 3 teaspoons baking powder
- 1 Tablespoon sugar
- 1 teaspoon salt
- 6 Tablespoons dry milk powder, which is best when camping
- 2 teaspoons black pepper
- 4 Tablespoons canola oil
- 1/2 cup shredded cheddar cheese
- 1 cup water
- 12 sausage patties
- 12 eggs

DIRECTIONS

1. In a medium bowl, whisk together flour, baking powder, sugar, salt, dry milk powder, black pepper and canola oil until well blended.

2. To mix the biscuits, pour dry mix into medium sized bowl and add 1/2 cup of water. Slowly add the remaining 1/2 cup of water 1 Tablespoon at a time until the biscuit mix is thick batter. Stir in cheddar cheese.

3. Set cast iron pan over medium heat and add oil to coat. Scoop biscuit mix by the scant 1/4 cup onto pan. Be sure you're only doing small batches at a time.

Allow to cook until first side is golden brown and flip once. Cook until biscuits are fluffy and cooked through.

4. Add sausage to a cold cast iron skillet and then set it over medium high heat. Cook until sausages are golden brown and cooked through, flipping once. Remove and set aside.

5. Cook eggs in cast iron skillet until desired doneness. Split biscuits in half and top with sausage and egg.

*Add ketchup or hot sauce if desired and place other half of biscuit on top.

RV Trashcan Hack

RVs can be cramped, and standard size household items rarely fit where you want them to. Need a trash can? Try using a dry food container that will fit snugly into a small space. Simply add a trash bag and you have an instant trash can. They fit perfect next to the toilet in the bathroom too!

A NOTE FROM TONYA

Thank y'all so much for this amazing journey we've been on with all the fun cozy mystery adventures! We've had so much fun and I can't wait to bring you a lot more of them. When I set out to write about them, I pulled from my experiences from camping, having a camper, and fond memories of camping.

Readers ask me if there's a real place like those in my books. Sadly, no. It's a combination of places I've stayed and would own if I could.

XOXO ~ Tonya

For a full reading order of Tonya Kappes's Novels, visit
Tonyakappes.com

BOOKS BY TONYA
SOUTHERN HOSPITALITY WITH A SMIDGEN OF HOMICIDE

Camper & Criminals Cozy Mystery Series

All is good in the camper-hood until a dead body shows up in the woods.

BEACHES, BUNGALOWS, AND BURGLARIES
DESERTS, DRIVING, & DERELICTS
FORESTS, FISHING, & FORGERY
CHRISTMAS, CRIMINALS, AND CAMPERS
MOTORHOMES, MAPS, & MURDER
CANYONS, CARAVANS, & CADAVERS
HITCHES, HIDEOUTS, & HOMICIDES
ASSAILANTS, ASPHALT & ALIBIS
VALLEYS, VEHICLES & VICTIMS
SUNSETS, SABBATICAL AND SCANDAL
TENTS, TRAILS AND TURMOIL
KICKBACKS, KAYAKS, AND KIDNAPPING
GEAR, GRILLS & GUNS
EGGNOG, EXTORTION, AND EVERGREEN
ROPES, RIDDLES, & ROBBERIES
PADDLERS, PROMISES & POISON
INSECTS, IVY, & INVESTIGATIONS
OUTDOORS, OARS, & OATH
WILDLIFE, WARRANTS, & WEAPONS
BLOSSOMS, BBQ, & BLACKMAIL
LANTERNS, LAKES, & LARCENY
JACKETS, JACK-O-LANTERN, & JUSTICE
SANTA, SUNRISES, & SUSPICIONS
VISTAS, VICES, & VALENTINES
ADVENTURE, ABDUCTION, & ARREST
RANGERS, RVS, & REVENGE

CAMPFIRES, COURAGE & CONVICTS
TRAPPING, TURKEY & THANKSGIVING
GIFTS, GLAMPING & GLOCKS
ZONING, ZEALOTS, & ZIPLINES
HAMMOCKS, HANDGUNS, & HEARSAY
QUESTIONS, QUARRELS, & QUANDARY
WITNESS, WOODS, & WEDDING
ELVES, EVERGREENS, & EVIDENCE
MOONLIGHT, MARSHMALLOWS, & MANSLAUGHTER
BONFIRE, BACKPACKS, & BRAWLS

Killer Coffee Cozy Mystery Series

Welcome to the Bean Hive Coffee Shop where the gossip is just as hot as the coffee.

SCENE OF THE GRIND
MOCHA AND MURDER
FRESHLY GROUND MURDER
COLD BLOODED BREW
DECAFFEINATED SCANDAL
A KILLER LATTE
HOLIDAY ROAST MORTEM
DEAD TO THE LAST DROP
A CHARMING BLEND NOVELLA (CROSSOVER WITH MAGICAL CURES MYSTERY)
FROTHY FOUL PLAY
SPOONFUL OF MURDER
BARISTA BUMP-OFF
CAPPUCCINO CRIMINAL
MACCHIATO MURDER

Holiday Cozy Mystery Series

BOOKS BY TONYA

CELEBRATE GOOD CRIMES!

FOUR LEAF FELONY
MOTHER'S DAY MURDER
A HALLOWEEN HOMICIDE
NEW YEAR NUISANCE
CHOCOLATE BUNNY BETRAYAL
FOURTH OF JULY FORGERY
SANTA CLAUSE SURPRISE
APRIL FOOL'S ALIBI

Kenni Lowry Mystery Series

Mysteries so delicious it'll make your mouth water and leave you hankerin' for more.

FIXIN' TO DIE
SOUTHERN FRIED
AX TO GRIND
SIX FEET UNDER
DEAD AS A DOORNAIL
TANGLED UP IN TINSEL
DIGGIN' UP DIRT
BLOWIN' UP A MURDER
HEAVENS TO BRIBERY

Magical Cures Mystery Series

Welcome to Whispering Falls where magic and mystery collide.

A CHARMING CRIME
A CHARMING CURE
A CHARMING POTION (novella)
A CHARMING WISH

A CHARMING SPELL
A CHARMING MAGIC
A CHARMING SECRET
A CHARMING CHRISTMAS (novella)
A CHARMING FATALITY
A CHARMING DEATH (novella)
A CHARMING GHOST
A CHARMING HEX
A CHARMING VOODOO
A CHARMING CORPSE
A CHARMING MISFORTUNE
A CHARMING BLEND (CROSSOVER WITH A KILLER COFFEE COZY)
A CHARMING DECEPTION

Mail Carrier Cozy Mystery Series

Welcome to Sugar Creek Gap where more than the mail is being delivered.

STAMPED OUT
ADDRESS FOR MURDER
ALL SHE WROTE
RETURN TO SENDER
FIRST CLASS KILLER
POST MORTEM
DEADLY DELIVERY
RED LETTER SLAY

About Tonya

Tonya has written over 100 novels, all of which have graced numerous bestseller lists, including the USA Today. Best known for stories charged with emotion and humor and filled with flawed characters, her novels have garnered reader praise and glowing critical reviews. She lives with her husband and a very spoiled rescue cat named Ro. Tonya grew up in the small southern Kentucky town of Nicholasville. Now that her four boys are grown men, Tonya writes full-time in her camper she calls her SHAMPER (she-camper).

Learn more about her be sure to check out her website tonyakappes.com. Find her on Facebook, Twitter, BookBub, and Instagram

Sign up to receive her newsletter, where you'll get free books, exclusive bonus content, and news of her releases and sales.

If you liked this book, please take a few minutes to leave a review now! Authors (Tonya included) really appreciate this, and it helps draw more readers to books they might like. Thanks!